"My dog was on the wrong end of a very sudden, very ugly dispute with a fierce pit bull that must have gotten loose in the neighborhood."

She continued, "We were taking a late-night walk and I think that Charlotte was trying to protect me. It all happened so fast, I didn't realize that anything was going on until I heard this awful barking and crying coming from Charlotte."

Fearing the worst, Sam asked, "And where's your dog now?"

"I put her into my car and drove over here. That's how I got all this blood on me," the woman told him, waving her hand at the front of her shirt. "I'm sorry to wake you up in the middle of the night like this, but someone I know gave me your name and address and said you were really good with dogs." She added, "I'm new here and I had nowhere to go." She flashed an apologetic look at him. He caught himself thinking that he had never had an apology look quite as good before.

Dear Reader,

Well, we're back, this time with a brand-new series revolving around the Sterling Brothers (and their father), five men born between eighteen months and two years apart. Shortly after the youngest was born, their mother died as a result of a car accident. At a loss, their father, with the help of his late wife's best friend, found a nanny to help care for the boys as if they were her own. She helped raise them and educate them (rather than just indulge them). Consequently, the boys grew up smart and educated as well as able to do things (they cooked as a way of honoring their mother, who loved to cook).

Their father, Sanford, was lost without his beloved wife, Shirley, but he found a way to keep going and make sure that his sons grew up educated and provided for. Thanks to their nanny, Randi, the boys never sat on their hands. The oldest, Samuel, is a veterinarian; the next in line, Simon, is a very serious divorce lawyer who does not believe in love because of what he has to deal with; Scott, the middle son, is an investment counselor and takes care of the family's finances; Sebastian, the next to youngest, is brilliant, having gotten his degrees in literature and become a college professor before he turned twenty; and Sean, the youngest and most likely the handsomest of the lot, managed to talk their father into taking him on as his partner despite not wanting his son to be part of a construction business.

The theme behind the books is getting his sons matched up so they could enjoy the sort of happiness that he, Sanford, did.

I hope I succeed in entertaining you, and from the bottom of my heart, I wish you someone to love who loves you back.

With all good thoughts,

Marie Ferrarella

THE BACHELOR'S MATCHMAKER

MARIE FERRARELLA

Harlequin
SPECIAL EDITION

Recycling programs for this product may not exist in your area.

ISBN-13: 978-1-335-40194-6

The Bachelor's Matchmaker

For questions and comments about the quality of this book, please contact us at CustomerService@Harlequin.com.

Harlequin Enterprises ULC
22 Adelaide St. West, 41st Floor
Toronto, Ontario M5H 4E3, Canada
www.Harlequin.com

Printed in Lithuania

USA TODAY bestselling and RITA® Award–winning author **Marie Ferrarella** has written more than three hundred books for Harlequin, some under the name Marie Nicole. Her romances are beloved by fans worldwide. Visit her website, marieferrarella.com.

Books by Marie Ferrarella

Harlequin Special Edition

Matchmaking Mamas

Diamond in the Ruff
Dating for Two
Wish Upon a Matchmaker
Ten Years Later...
A Perfectly Imperfect Match
Once Upon a Matchmaker

Harlequin Romantic Suspense

Cavanaugh Justice

Cavanaugh Vanguard
Cavanaugh Cowboy
Cavanaugh's Missing Person
Cavanaugh Stakeout
Cavanaugh in Plain Sight
Cavanaugh Justice: The Baby Trail
Cavanaugh Justice: Serial Affair
Cavanaugh Justice: Deadly Chase
Cavanaugh Justice: Up Close and Deadly
Cavanaugh Justice: Detecting a Killer
Cavanaugh Justice: Cold Case Squad

The Coltons of New York

Colton's Unusual Suspect

Visit the Author Profile page at Harlequin.com for more titles.

TO

My Editor,

Patience Bloom,

Who Is the Living Embodiment

Of Just That,

Patience,

With a Dose of Love

Thrown In,

I Will Always Be Eternally Grateful

We Crossed Each Other's Paths

Prologue

Sanford Sterling sat in the trailer he had parked at the newest construction site he had set up. He felt incredibly lost and alone. This sensation was nothing new. It came whenever he was alone with his thoughts, looking at the framed photograph he kept on his desk of his late wife. He was contemplating what his life had become in the years since Shirley had died as a result of a car accident, which had left him with their five sons to raise—two of whom were too young at the time when she died to even remember what she had been like.

"Oh, Lord, Shirley, you have no idea how much I wish you were here," he told the woman in the photograph. "Our boys need to settle down, to get married and start their own families. They need your help—*I* need your help. I lucked out when I found you."

He sighed deeply, remembering the day he first saw her. She had walked into his second-period English class on a Tuesday morning in eighth grade. He fell in love with her right then and there—and they had been together ever since. Until the day she had been taken from him. The resulting wound was still fresh even after all these years.

"I want our boys to feel that sort of luck coursing through their veins, but how on earth do I manage to do that for them? I need your help, Shirley. I really, really need you next to me. I don't want to guide our sons into making a mistake, marrying the wrong woman. Otherwise, they'll be sorry for the rest of their lives. I've never been able to even get them to find time for any serious dating." Sanford sighed, shaking his head. "They've always been too focused on getting their degrees and starting their careers. That much I've accomplished." He had a feeling that had been because Shirley was looking down at her sons and guiding their every move.

But this was too much to hope for—and how could he even be able to get all five of his sons to pair up with the right women? The best dating advice he had to offer was "follow your heart."

Sanford combed his fingers through his hair, frustrated and at a complete loss. "Oh, Shirley, I need you now more than ever. The *boys* need you," he whispered into the shadows.

And then suddenly, just like that, it came to him. The answer. From out of the past.

Maizie.

Maizie Sommers had been Shirley's close friend in high school as well as her maid of honor at their wedding. And, just as important, she had been the one who had helped him find a nanny to watch over the boys so he was able to go back to work, to earn a living and provide for his family.

That hadn't been easy, either, but Maizie was right there beside him, despite her busy schedule, weeding out potential candidates for the position of the boys' nanny, promising him he was going to get through this, assuring him that he *had* to get through this for Shirley's sake. And ultimately telling him that if there was absolutely *anything* she could do for him, she would.

For Shirley's sake.

And that was when he suddenly remembered. Aside from being a successful real estate agent, on the side, Maizie also ran a matchmaking service with two of her best friends. She took no money for it, instead gathering a sense of pride and feeling of accomplishment from the matchup.

That was his answer, Sanford realized.

"Matchmaking service," he said out loud, happy for once that his youngest son and business partner was not on-site with him. "Of course. Boy, talk about being thick," he murmured, shaking his head.

The first opportunity he got, he planned on paying Maizie a visit and laying this new dilemma he found himself facing at her feet. He needed help, and he didn't mind admitting it. This needed a woman's touch, he thought.

"Brace yourself, Sam," he said to his firstborn,

the one he was planning on matching up first. "Your fancy-free days are about to come to an end."

He was that confident that Maizie was about to find someone for Sam.

Now that he thought about it, he had heard good things about the enduring matches that Maizie and her friends had made in the last fifteen years. It gave him hope.

"My sweet boys," he said to the image he had in his heart of his sons. "Your lives are about to change—for the better," he said with certainty.

He decided that Sam, as his oldest, was going to be first. It only seemed fair to go that route. He had a feeling that Shirley would definitely approve of this move.

As soon as he was alone—and able—he placed a call to Maizie. It turned out to be the following day. Since she was successful in both her real estate business and this matchmaking, he had a feeling that he would need an appointment to see Maizie in a timely fashion.

Not that the woman would put obstacles in his way, but he wanted to pay her the courtesy of going to her on her timetable rather than his own, even though he was exceedingly busy 24/7.

Maizie picked up her phone on the third ring. "Maizie Sommers, how may I help you?"

He would have recognized that bright, chipper

voice anywhere. "Maizie, this is Sanford Sterling. Would you be available to meet with me tomorrow?"

It had been several years. "Sandy, is that really you?" she cried, clearly stunned. And then she immediately asked, "Is anything wrong?"

The last time they had spoken was at Sean's college graduation. To her credit as a good friend of both parents, Maizie had attended all five of their sons' college graduations, which was why he felt he could count on her to help him to successfully match up his sons.

"No, as a matter of fact, there isn't," Sanford told her. "But once again, I find myself in need of your very unique services."

He imagined Maizie making herself comfortable. "I'm listening. What can I do?"

He took a breath, launching into the reason for his call. "You once told me that you and your two friends had dipped your toes in matchmaking waters. Are you still treading water?"

"Not for a while now," she admitted. "But the girls and I are ready and eager to get back into it. You're not looking, are you?" she asked incredulously.

No one loved their late wife as much as Sandy loved Shirley. "No, not me, but it's time for the boys to find their soulmates. I hear you're really good at that sort of matchup."

He could hear the smile in Maizie's voice. "As a matter of fact, we are. Why don't you come down to the office the first opportunity you get, and we'll discuss the particulars?" she suggested.

"Tomorrow morning too soon?" he asked her.

"Tomorrow's perfect, Sandy. I look forward to seeing you," she told him. "How about ten?"

This was going to be good. "Sounds perfect," he told her.

"I certainly hope so" was Maizie's response.

The shopping center where Maizie's real estate agency was located had changed somewhat since Sanford had seen it last. It had been built up over the years, even though it continued to maintain its warm, friendly, welcoming appearance.

As he pulled into the lot, he felt as if he had butterflies in his stomach, a strange feeling for a grown man to have, he thought. But this was important. Very important, he told himself. If this visit went well, the ones that would follow would, too.

Parking his vehicle, he made his way over to the recently renovated real estate building. It looked inviting, he thought. That was a good sign. Taking a deep breath at the front door, he knocked once, opened it, then went inside.

There was one person inside. It wasn't a client. He flashed a quick smile in greeting, then nodded.

The woman came straight for him, her arms outstretched. "Sanford?" she asked.

"Maizie, you haven't aged a day since I last saw you at Sean's graduation," he told her.

"And you are still spreading it as thick as you ever did," Maizie said with a laugh, planting a kiss on Sanford's cheek. "How have you been, Sandy?"

"Busy." And then he admitted, "Lonely."

"Do you still have Sunday dinners at the house the way you all used to?" she asked him.

He nodded. "It's a tribute to Shirley."

Maizie smiled broadly. "She would have been very proud. Come, sit," she urged. "So are the boys ready for something serious?"

"Absolutely," he answered. "And I realize that I'm just not any good at matchups. But word on the street is that you and your two friends are extremely good at it."

"Well, I don't mean to get your hopes up," Maizie confessed, "but so far, my friends and I have been batting a thousand."

"I'd say that's pretty damn good," Sanford told her. "Do you think you could do it a few more times?"

Her smile all but lit up the room. "Absolutely," she told him. "I just need to ask you a few preliminary questions. But first, how is everyone?"

"Busy," he said again. "That's the problem. The boys are too busy at the moment to do the ordinary things that men their age normally do. That's why I need you, Maizie. They just don't seem to be able to find the time to sow their oats, wild or otherwise.

They seem obsessed with laying the foundations of their various careers. Sam is a veterinarian, Simon is a divorce lawyer, Sebastian—"

Maizie held up her hand, stopping Sanford mid-sentence. "You don't have to go through all their vocations. I was there at each of their graduations, remember?" she reminded her late friend's husband. "I can take it from here," she assured him. "Are they happy in their chosen fields?"

"They never gave me any reason to doubt that they were very happy," he told her.

Maizie frowned. "Not exactly a ringing endorsement."

"They're not exactly a talkative bunch, at least not around me," Sanford told her.

"Boys have trouble making their feelings known around their father, especially when he sacrificed so much for them," Maizie pointed out. She made a notation on her folder, then looked up. "Are they still as handsome as ever?"

He felt the usual fondness whenever he thought of his boys. "I'm sure that their mother would say that they are."

Maizie flashed a warm smile at him. "Just like their father," she pointed out.

Sanford gave her a look. "I'm not fishing for a compliment."

"I know that," the potential matchmaker told him. "You were never that vain. That was one of the things that Shirley liked about you. She would have approved of you trying to match up your sons to their potential soulmates. So, is Sam dedicated to his vocation?"

"If he could, he would care for animals for free," he told Maizie.

"Selfless and dedicated. There's a lot of his mother and his father in him," she told Sanford.

"But I know my limitations, which is why I've come to you for help," he told her.

Maizie nodded. "Tell me, do I have a time limit on this?"

"Just sometime before I die would be nice, although I need to tell you that I would like to be able to enjoy my grandkids," he told her.

Maizie smiled, probably thinking of her own grandchildren. "Oh, they are just the very best," she assured him. "You get to play with little people and enjoy them without worrying that you're doing things wrong. Because you know you're not." She patted her friend on his broad shoulder. "Smile, Sandy. It's going to be all right, I promise," she said, leaning over the desk and squeezing his hand. "Are there any physical preferences? You know, blonde, brunette, tall, short, that sort of thing."

"Only that she's breathing," Sanford specified.

Maizie nodded, lips pursed as if to keep from laughing. "Definitely breathing," she agreed. She leaned back in her chair, reviewing the notes that she had taken. "Well, I think I have everything I need. I take it you want to match up all of your sons?"

"Most definitely yes," he answered.

"In order?" She knew him well.

"Well, I think that would only be fair," he pointed out.

Maizie nodded. "Wouldn't want any of the boys to think that you're playing favorites," she said, "putting one above the other."

"Just like doing things in their proper order, that's all," Sanford said. "I always have. Will that be a problem?"

"Not for me," she answered. "If we find someone more suited to one of the other brothers, I'll just make a note to get back to the woman at a later date—unless, of course, there's a danger of losing the woman, and if we come up against that, then we'll take the proper precautions."

Sanford smiled. "That's why I came to you, Maizie. You know how to juggle things and keep all the balls up in the air at the same time. If you need anything to make this happen, just let me know," Sanford said. "Also, that goes for any payments."

"Payments?" she questioned, looking at him oddly.

"For possibly the initial outlay," Sanford specified.

She was still confused by his meaning. "Such as?"

"I'll leave that to your imagination," Sanford told her.

She flashed a smile at him. "Not to worry," she answered. "I have plenty to work on in my notes. Let me talk to my friends Theresa Manetti and Cecilia Parnell. We'll put our heads together and see if we can come up with a good candidate for Sam. There'll be a good backstory—all true," she specified. "And once we find the proper candidate for Sam, we'll go from there."

"She needs to be an animal lover," Sanford told her.

"Most assuredly. I wasn't born yesterday, Sandy. This is for my friend's son—as well as my godson," she said. She saw the look on Sanford's face. "You forgot that part, didn't you? Well, I didn't. I remember how he wiggled and wriggled as I held him while he was being baptized. Out of all the matchups I plan to make, Sam will be my very best," she promised. "You have my word on it."

Sanford took heart from the look on Maizie's face. "You've made me very happy, Maizie," he told her as he rose to his feet.

"Good. Then I'll get in contact with you once all the pieces come together," she told him. "My advice to you is to prepare for a wedding."

"You can be that sure of the outcome?" Sanford questioned.

Maizie flashed a bright smile at her friend. "Oh, I can be that sure," she told him with unshakable certainty.

Sanford smiled at Maizie. "Then I'll go home and wait for your call."

Her eyes sparkled. "You do that," she encouraged her friend.

She couldn't wait to call her friends with the news. They were going to be thrilled.

Chapter One

Theresa Manetti and Cecilia Parnell were already waiting next to Maizie's front door when she pulled into her driveway. Both women had expectant expressions on their faces when they saw her approaching.

"You're early," Maizie called out to her friends as she walked up to them.

"You're late," Celia countered with her hand on her hip. "Okay, we're here. So what's up?"

Maizie didn't answer the woman immediately. Instead, she waited until she unlocked the front door, pausing for dramatic effect. Theresa and Celia were used to her behavior. They had known each other for years.

Maizie, Theresa and Celia had a friendship that dated all the way back to the third grade. It was a continuous, lifelong friendship. The three of them had gone through absolutely *everything* together over the years. That included weddings, the births of their children and, sadly, the deaths of their husbands.

They had also, in desperation and unbeknownst to their children, played matchmakers for their children. The secret romantic matches involved Maizie's pediatrician daughter, Nikki; Celia's private investigator daughter; and Theresa's son and daughter, who were both attorneys-at-law. As a matter of fact, their matchmaking efforts had gone so well that after discussing the matter at length, the three friends had decided to branch out and undertake making further matches.

But due to extenuating circumstances, things had slowed down of late, and the friends had been forced to pay more attention to other aspects of their lives.

Until, Maizie thought with a smile, Sanford Sterling had walked into her office today.

Closing the door behind Theresa, Maizie paused once again, then announced, "Ladies, I am happy to tell you that we are finally back in business."

Celia looked at her friend, puzzled. "What do you mean, 'we're back in business'?" she asked as she unbuttoned her sweater and took it off. She placed it over the back of her chair. "We were never out of business, not in all these years."

It was true. Since they had each begun their separate business endeavors, their businesses had been growing steadily. And there was a reason for that. While other people were going on vacations and eventually contemplating the benefits of retirement, that sort of thing never crossed the three friends' minds. Never once. They far preferred working and reaping the fruits of their labors.

Bemused, Theresa tapped Celia on the shoulder. When her friend turned to look at her, Theresa told her, "I don't think that Maizie is talking about the kind of business that yields a monetary profit. I think that she is talking about an emotional one."

Maizie laughed. "Give that lady a cigar," she said, going to the kitchen. She took out the refreshments from the refrigerator that she had previously prepared during her lunch break.

Celia didn't bother attempting to mask her surprise. "You're kidding. Considering the last few years we have all gone through, I was beginning to think we had all just moved on when it came to dealing with people's romances. Nice to know that the matchmaking dream continues."

"Yes, isn't it?" Maizie said, delighted. Picking up the tray, she carried it into the family room and set it on the card table where they usually played their very low-key poker games.

"So, tell us," Celia urged. "Who is it? Anyone we know?"

"As a matter of fact," Maizie told them with a wide smile, "it is."

"Considering the number of people we know when you combine all our various acquaintances together, that does account for an awful lot of people," Theresa noted, her eyes sweeping over her two friends.

Since having someone come to them for their matchmaking services was such a rare event these days, Maizie decided that she could be forgiven for stretching this out just a little more. "This is someone from a long time ago."

Celia shook her head. "Still not narrowing it down enough," she told Maizie. She gave her friend a scrutinizing look. "Are you going to make us play twenty questions?"

Maizie smiled warmly at Celia. "Only if you want to."

The two other women exchanged looks, then simultaneously said, "We don't want to."

At which point Celia followed up their declaration with one of her own. "Give," she ordered Maizie, "or things just might have to get ugly."

"Heaven forbid," Maizie said. "All right, do you ladies remember Sanford Sterling?" she asked, giving each of her friends a scrutinizing look.

"That poor man who lost his wife and was left with five little sons to raise?" Theresa asked. "Of course we remember him. We all went to school together back in the day. You were Shirley and Sanford's maid of honor."

"I can remember those boys used to just love playing with the train sets that I gave them," Celia recalled fondly.

"Well, the boys are not playing with trains anymore," Maizie informed her friends.

Theresa's eyes opened wide as she clearly realized

what Maizie was telling them. "Oh my God, do you mean to tell me that that much time has gone by?"

Maizie nodded. "I mean to tell you that that much time has gone by," she confirmed.

"Wow," Celia said in disbelief. Reaching across the table, she picked up a homemade mint fudge brownie that Maizie had made on her lunch break. It turned out to be the perfect way to celebrate this piece of unexpected good news.

"My sentiments exactly," Theresa agreed, responding to Celia's "wow."

"How could they have possibly gotten so much older? I certainly haven't," Theresa maintained with a smile.

Celia laughed. "You keep telling yourself that, Theresa."

"Why shouldn't she?" Maizie asked, feigning surprise. "We haven't."

"Deal," Celia instructed, pointing to the deck in front of Maizie. She waited until full hands were distributed all around. "So, when do we get together with Sanford so we can pin down all the particulars?"

Theresa asked another pertinent question: "Which son does Sanford want us to find a soulmate for?"

"I got the impression that Sandy wanted to do these matchups in order. You know, not putting one son in front of the other because he didn't feel it was right." Maizie thought that was exceedingly fair. "He mentioned that he wanted us to find a wife for Sam first."

Theresa nodded her approval. "Sam," she repeated. "Did he happen to tell you what Sam is doing these days?" That was a usual question that they asked for matchups, but admittedly it had been a while since they had done this.

"He didn't have to. I know what Sam's field is," Maizie said as she put down three cards and held up the corresponding fingers for Celia's benefit.

Theresa sighed. "Of course you do," she said, rolling her eyes. "What was I thinking?"

"Don't crack wise, Theresa," Celia reprimanded their friend. "You know Maizie doesn't like you getting ahead of her story until she's ready." Celia's smile widened until it all but took in the entire room, lighting it up. "I can't tell you how good this makes me feel," she confided. "It feels like it's been forever since we brought love into someone's life."

Theresa frowned ever so slightly. "Don't jinx it, Celia."

Maizie looked at Theresa over the top of her cards. "Since when did you get so superstitious?" she asked.

"Since we've never had a single failure in all the time we've been bringing couples together. I mean, think of the odds. I have to admit that I'm afraid it's just a matter of time."

"What I would rather think is that the next matchup is going to be our next big success," Maizie said.

Celia laughed as she shook her head. "I guess you really are an optimist, aren't you, Maizie?"

Maizie just smiled at her friend. "I find that being an optimist is the only way to survive in this world," she responded.

Theresa closed her eyes and nodded. "Amen to that."

"So." Celia looked from one friend to the other. "Do we have any idea what Sam's type is?"

"Quite frankly, from what Sandy told me during the course of my interview, he's been too busy working and building up his veterinary business to focus on a type," Maizie answered.

"But he is an animal lover," Celia said, making the assumption.

"Oh, that's putting it mildly," Maizie confirmed.

Theresa nodded, clearly organizing her thoughts. "So, we look into pairing him up with another animal lover."

"It couldn't be just that simple," Celia said. "There has to be more to it than that."

Theresa laughed. "I'm not suggesting that the perfect match has to be able to swing through the trees and hang upside down from one to qualify as Sam Sterling's love match."

Maizie smiled at the simplistic description. Things were never that easy. "Did I mention that Sam has a soft spot in his heart for dogs and cats, with the occasional exotic bird thrown in?" she asked, her eyes crinkling as she grinned at her two friends.

"You did now," Celia replied.

"Sandy also mentioned that, in his opinion, Sam was somewhat overworked, devoting all his spare time to treating and caring for the animals, whether or not their owners are able to pay for his services immediately. As a matter of fact, as far as I know, the only time he does take off is for Sunday dinners."

"Sunday dinners?" Celia repeated, curious for more information.

Maizie nodded. "That was something Shirley started because Sandy was so busy building up his company he hardly had any time for his growing family. She insisted that he take a few hours off at least on Sundays so that the family could have dinner together. From what I gathered, Sandy complained about it, but the truth of it was, he could never say no to Shirley when it came to anything." She didn't give in to the sad feeling that was washing over her. "Sandy told me," she continued, "that after his wife passed away, he and the boys continued the Sunday dinner tradition in order to honor Shirley."

"I think that's really sweet," Theresa told her two friends.

Maizie nodded again. "That gives you some insight into the kind of young men we're dealing with. Apparently none of the boys have ever skipped out on Sunday dinners. They obviously know how much those dinners used to mean to their mother."

"Good for them," Theresa said, nodding her head in approval. "All right, for now we are going to be on the lookout for a bright young woman who has a weakness for working with animals and is in the market for a job. What do you think?" she asked.

Maizie laid out her winning hand on the table, smiled and declared, "Right."

Celia frowned. "How do you do that? Keep your mind on the conversation and still manage to win the hand that you're playing?" she wanted to know. "It doesn't seem very fair."

"It's called *multitasking*," Maizie told her friend.

"Don't feel bad," Theresa told Celia. "Maizie used to drive her husband crazy with that particular little talent of hers."

"I can see why," Celia said. "You know, I think I might have a candidate for this little matchup of ours." She smiled broadly at her friends. "As a matter of fact, I am sure of it. Give me until tomorrow to check this out." Her smile grew decidedly more pronounced.

"Oh, by all means, Celia, check away to your heart's content." Maizie looked first from one friend, then to the other, her heart all but glowing. "Ladies," she happily announced, "we are definitely back."

She could see that her friends agreed.

Chapter Two

"Good thing you don't expect me to just drop everything and cook for you," Sam Sterling said to the overly eager German shepherd shadowing his every step from the moment they walked in the house together. The large dog was dancing from one side to the other. "God, Rocky, I wish I had at least half of your energy. Well, actually," the veterinarian said, reconsidering his words, "I did. But that was much earlier this morning."

Sam sighed as he stopped in front of his refrigerator and took out a number of items packed away in plastic containers. He would combine several of them to create Rocky's evening meal.

The dog's name had been Rocky ever since she was a little thing at the local animal shelter almost four years ago. She had turned out to be a female, and Sam was all set to change her name when he adopted her, but he had reconsidered, thinking that changing her name might be confusing for the German shepherd. So he had, as his mother had been so fond of saying years ago, "left well enough alone."

Rocky's name was the first thing about her that strangers remarked on in surprise, and occasionally disbelief. It also allowed Sam to easily segue into stories about the dog's life, stories that he used to his advantage when it came to treating other ill pets.

But right about now, Sam just wanted to prepare Rocky's food, set it out on the kitchen floor, watch her polish it off and put the bowl in the sink. Right after that, he intended to stumble off to bed, with any luck, headfirst. Plans to eat dinner and catch a program that had aroused his curiosity earlier today had simply faded away. Sam really wasn't hungry any longer, and all he wanted to do was go to sleep and not have his mind challenged or even teased the slightest bit.

The vet paused for a moment to affectionately rub the shepherd's fur along her head and face. Rocky took this as a sign that her master wanted to play, but after the day that Sam had put in, nothing could have been further from the truth. She attempted to nip his hand and get him to chase her, but Sam didn't budge.

"Sorry, girl. I just don't have the strength to play with you tonight. Maybe we'll have more luck this Sunday. Or at least you will," he told the frisky dog.

If he didn't get her food ready, he was going to fall asleep right here where he stood, Sam thought. Forcing himself to move, he opened up the container of pumpkin filling, another container of boiled shredded chicken breasts, as well as shredded cheddar cheese and a small helping of dry dog food. He mixed it all together with a very small helping of the chicken broth he had used to prepare the chicken breasts.

"You realize that you're spoiling that animal," his brother Simon had accused more than once while observing him mixing a meal for Rocky.

Sam had not been moved by the accusation. Simon was a high-powered divorce lawyer who, as far as Sam was concerned, had shut his heart to everyone and everything except for their immediate family—and at times Sam wasn't all that convinced that Simon even allowed his family in.

"You know, it might do you some good to get yourself a pet and spoil it a little, too," Sam told his brother.

"And why would I want to do that?" Simon asked, keeping his distance from Sam's very animated pet.

"Might remind you to be human," Sam had told him.

But Simon had only shaken his head. "Being reminded of that fact only creates pain and disappointment. Trust me," he said wearily, "I know. Dealing with the people I deal with, I really know."

"Maybe you would have been happier if you became a farmer," Sam had quipped, even though he knew that wasn't really true. Sam knew that Simon was good at his chosen career.

"I'm plenty happy." Simon had all but growled his answer.

"Uh-huh," Sam had said, sounding sarcastic even to his ear.

Simon had frowned and then just sighed. "I take it you don't believe me."

It was hard for Sam not to laugh at that point. "So tell me, brother, what was your first clue?"

Simon waved his hand at his older brother, made a disparaging noise and then just walked away to join Sunday dinner, ending that conversation for the time being.

Recalling that now, Sam half smiled to himself.

For the most part, he got along well with all his brothers. He always had—as long as they weren't packed too tightly together and could make room for their differences. Otherwise, they could and most likely would get on each other's nerves. But he supposed when everything was all said and done, there was nothing really unusual about that among brothers.

Given any sort of emergency—*any* sort—all the brothers were there for one another. They always had been ever since they were very young. He realized, as time went on, being there for one another was a way to cope with the fact that their mother could no longer be there for them. Of course, they certainly couldn't make up for the fact that Shirley Sterling was gone, and she was never coming back. What really did help them deal with the situation was the memory that she had created and left behind for them in her wake.

Sam instinctively knew that if his mother were here right now, she would fuss over him, and he would be subjected to a kindly lecture that he needed to take care of himself and should not allow himself to get so worn out. But he couldn't back away from his work. Being dedicated to caring for animals usually yielded this sort of result, he thought. And truth be told, Sam wouldn't have it any other way.

With a strong wave of affection, Sam looked down at the German shepherd.

"C'mon, Rocky, time to eat your dinner so I can get some sleep, or I am going to leave you home tomorrow, and you can spend the day in the backyard, staring at the fence," he told her.

Whether or not his dog understood what he was saying—and if she did, whether she believed what he was saying to her—Sam knew it was just an empty threat. He would no more leave his dog alone in the backyard than he would drop her off in the forest for the day. He was merely talking so that Rocky would respond to the sound of his voice.

Mashing her dinner together, he placed the dog dish in front of her. He had barely pulled his hand back when the German shepherd made short work of what he had set before her.

"Maybe I should count all my fingers just to be sure I still have them," he quipped, looking down at his hand.

Rocky made a noise and looked up at her master

quizzically before very quickly polishing off the remainder of that evening's dinner.

As much as he pretended to be stern about this feeding ritual, seeing Rocky enjoy her food warmed Sam's heart. Almost four years had passed since she had accidentally come into his life and he had taken her into both his heart and his home, but he could remember meeting her as clearly as if it had all taken place just yesterday.

One of the people who ran the shelter had called and asked him to come by. There was an aging spaniel with a growth on his neck that needed to be looked at. Sam had treated the dog the way he always did, charging the shelter only what it cost him for the medication. He hadn't charged for his time, saying that his reward was the satisfaction he derived from seeing the animal get well.

While he was working with the spaniel, a floppy German shepherd had somehow gotten out of her cage and began to follow him around. When one of the caretakers caught her and returned her to her cage, the shepherd had cried so much trying and failing to get to him that she was virtually impossible to ignore. So when he finished sewing up where the spaniel had managed to injure himself, Sam turned his attention to the nosy German shepherd.

"What's the shepherd's name?" he asked. The first thing the local shelter did with new animals was name them.

"Rocky," the attendant informed him.

"Oh, like the fighter in the movie," he remembered commenting with a grin.

The attendant had laughed and said, "No, not quite."

He hadn't seen why that was funny until he allowed the shepherd to climb onto his lap and he began to pet it. That was when he noticed Rocky was female. He still hadn't thought about adopting her until she started crying pathetically again when he tried to walk away. After the third time, Sam decided this had to be some sort of omen.

"I guess this means I should take her home with me," he said to the attendant.

As it turned out, this was the attendant's first pairing of a stray with a potential candidate. Then, because Sam had done so much free work for them, the shelter waived the usual adoption fees.

"And the perfect union was born," Sam murmured now, looking at Rocky as he relived that earlier time. He was sitting on the family room floor, petting Rocky as she made short work of her freshly filled water dish. Or what had been a freshly filled water dish a few minutes ago.

"Okay, young lady. It's one last run in the backyard for you. Do what you need to do and empty yourself out and then it's bedtime for you, Rocky." He looked down at the dog. "Have I made myself clear, young lady?"

Rocky barked in response.

He knew there were those people who maintained that all conversations with pets were one-sided, but no one would ever convince him that Rocky didn't understand what he was saying to her, no matter how firmly they voiced their opinion.

Sam pulled himself up to his feet. "Well, I don't know about you, girl, but I am definitely ready to call it a day and go to bed," he told the dog. "I feel like I've put in at least thirty-six hours straight."

Rocky cocked her head at him, and he could swear she was trying to make sense of what he was telling her.

"I know, I know, I'm exaggerating, but I really feel that way. I didn't even get to stop for lunch today, and if I don't crawl into bed in the next few minutes, my battery is going to totally die, and I'm going to be good for absolutely nothing come morning."

After he let Rocky out one last time and the dog returned, Sam started up the stairs with Rocky lumbering right next to him.

"Yes, yes," Sam murmured as he took the stairs at a far slower pace than his pet did, "you've heard all this before. Well, I'm sorry, but I'm not up to being clever and interesting after being on my feet and on call all these endless hours. Feel free to run away and find another master if you think you can do better."

Sam paused at the top of the stairs to look at her. She remained where she was, looking up at him, making no indication that she was about to go anywhere.

"No, I didn't think so," he said as he walked into his bedroom.

Rocky was less than a beat behind him. She raced him for the bed and sprawled out on it several seconds before he could reach it.

Sam didn't remember crashing onto the mattress. And he certainly didn't remember closing his eyes. But he must have, because the world around him faded away and darkness descended. It was definitely time to sleep—and he did.

Chapter Three

Sam's eyes flew open.

At first he thought he'd just imagined the noise. Maybe he was having an exceedingly vivid dream that refused to subside and present itself calmly within the scope of his day-to-day world.

There was absolutely nothing calm about the banging noise penetrating his brain and vibrating throughout his body.

What finally convinced him it wasn't a dream was Rocky leaping up from bed and running to the noise at the front door. Sam didn't even bother to pause and stretch. Instead, he was on his feet, heading toward the door to discover who was pounding on it. And, more important, why.

"Now what?" Sam mumbled, trying his best to get the sleep out of his eyes while attempting to get his brain in gear. By the time he did, he had reached the door, right behind his overly anxious German shepherd. "Calm down, Rocky. Burglars aren't going to pound on the door. They try to sneak in."

Rocky didn't behave as if she believed him.

Grabbing the shepherd around the neck, Sam really wished he had left her collar on so he had something to hang on to. He tried to soothe the animal as best he could as he reached for the front door. "Calm down, Rocky, stay calm," he said in a soft singsong.

At first, he opened the front door just a crack. This was an exceedingly safe city and had been so for years, but there was always a first time, he thought. But as soon as Sam opened the door enough to look out, Rocky seemed to calm down. At least to some degree.

It seemed to Sam that his pet was reacting to the young woman standing on the other side of his threshold, a very attractive, worried-looking young woman.

It was the middle of the night and fairly dark, so it took Sam several moments to realize that there was blood on the front of the woman's shirt.

Sam came to instantly, immediately concerned. "Are you hurt?" he asked. He opened his front door wide, issuing a silent invitation to her to come into the house.

The young blonde shook her head.

Rocky, Sam noticed, had stopped barking altogether. Instead, his ordinarily protective pet was sniffing around the intruder and had obviously made a guess as to where the blood on the woman's clothes had come from.

"It's not my blood," she told the vet she had gotten out of bed. "It's Charlotte's."

Sam peered behind the woman as well as around her. There was no sign of this so-called Charlotte as far as he could see. One hand on the doorknob, he began to close the door, still keeping an eye on both his dog and the noisy visitor who had disturbed his sleep.

"And Charlotte is?" he asked, pinning the woman with an inquiring look.

"My dog that was on the wrong end of a sudden, ugly dispute with a fierce pit bull that must have gotten loose in the neighborhood," she told Sam. "We were taking a late-night walk, and I think that Charlotte was trying to protect me. It all happened so fast, I didn't realize anything was going on until I heard this awful barking and crying coming from Charlotte."

Fearing the worst, Sam asked, "And where's your dog now?"

"I put her in my car and drove over here. That's how I got all this blood on me," the woman told him, waving her hand at the front of her shirt. "I'm sorry to wake you up in the middle of the night like this, but someone I know gave me your name and address and said you were really good with dogs," she explained, adding, "I'm new here, and I had nowhere to go." She flashed an apologetic look at him. He caught himself thinking that he had never had an apology look quite as good before. "I'm very sorry for all this."

"No reason to apologize," Sam told her. First things first, he thought. "You said your dog was in your car?"

The blonde nodded and immediately turned on her heel. She headed back toward a vehicle parked next to the curb. "Yes, she's right out here, Dr. Sterling," the young woman said as she led him to the beige late-model sports car.

A streetlight at the end of the block helped illuminate the area and allowed Sam to see just where he was going. More important, it allowed him to see the sad-looking, mangled creature lying across the Honda's back seat.

The dog attempted to bark at Sam as he approached. It was easy to see that the animal was afraid as well as bleeding.

"What's the dog's name again?" he asked the woman.

"Her name is Charlotte," she answered, opening the right rear door.

The dog was cowering, all but sinking into the back seat.

"Hello, Charlotte. I see you've gotten yourself into a little trouble," Sam said softly, keeping his voice low so as not to frighten the wounded dog. "Why don't you come with me, and I'll see what we can do to get you all cleaned up and to stop that bleeding?"

The miniature collie looked up at Sam with a pitiful expression in her eyes.

"I don't think she can walk," Charlotte's owner told Sam. She wasn't going for pity—she seemed to be genuinely concerned.

Sam regarded the wounded collie with kindness. "I wasn't planning on making Charlotte walk."

With that, Sam leaned into the vehicle, and very carefully and with maximum tenderness, he slowly took the animal out of the car and into his arms, being very careful not to hurt her in any way.

"What can I do?" the dog's owner asked as she shifted from foot to foot.

He glanced in her direction for a moment. "Honestly? Right now, my suggestion is that you try not to get in my way." Despite her diminutive appearance, the dog was rather solidly built. "Did you actually carry this dog and put her into your car?"

"I'm stronger than I look," she told him.

Sam was far from being a weakling, but he felt he had to move very carefully not to drop or jostle the dog in his arms. "You'd have to be," he told her.

"You know how sometimes you hear stories about a parent tapping into a wave of almost superhuman strength that allows them to do things people wouldn't think they could normally do?" she asked.

He was vaguely aware of that sort of thing happening sometimes. "Yes."

"Well, this was one of those times. Charlotte was injured and bleeding, and I just couldn't leave her like that."

Sam could definitely understand that. "You had no one to ask to help you?"

"I'm relatively new here," she repeated. "I don't know anyone in the area very well, and I wasn't about to impose."

"And yet you came pounding on my door," he pointed out, slowly making his way back to his home with the woman's injured pet.

"Extenuating circumstances," she said. "I wouldn't have normally done that."

Sam nodded. He could feel the dog breathing very hard as he held the animal against his chest. "I see your point."

"Is your shepherd in danger of running off?" she asked, looking at Rocky. The dog was dancing from foot to foot in front of them.

"Rocky knows better than that," he told her. "I made sure she was trained well before I allowed her to have this much freedom."

Charlotte's owner appeared uncertain as her eyes shifted toward the shepherd. "Far be it from me to argue with you," she told him. She held her breath as she followed her injured pet into Sam's clinic. "I can't tell you how my heart stopped when I saw that dog charging at Charlotte with those awful teeth bared. I threw dirt into his face to distract him, but it didn't even faze him. For a minute, I was afraid that the dog was going to rip Charlotte limb from limb. That's why I have all this blood on me."

Sam began to shoulder open his door. The woman quickly stepped up and pushed it open for them. "Thanks." He looked her over for a second. "Is any of that blood yours?"

"Honestly?" she asked. "I really don't know. It might be. Things happened so fast, and I managed to get the pit bull away from Charlotte by throwing a bunch of rocks at it, but the pit bull did try to bite me a couple of times. There's no scarier sound than hearing those sharp teeth clamping down next to you."

"When I finish with Charlotte, let me take a look at your arms and all the places you might be bleeding," he told her, nodding at her exposed skin.

"Okay, but Charlotte first," the pet owner insisted.

"That's what I just said," he told her, leading the way farther into the animal clinic. Sam indicated the exam table on one side of the room. "I'm going to put her down here. I think she will feel better if she sees you standing beside her."

"I won't get in your way?" the woman asked, concerned.

"I think you know enough not to do that," Sam told Charlotte's owner. He looked down at his pet. "Rocky, go wait in your play area."

As the woman watched in fascination, Rocky trotted off into a back room. Sam turned his attention to his patient. "Okay, pretty girl, let's see what that big bad pit bull did to you."

The wounded animal cried as Sam very carefully examined the gashes and tears along her skin.

"I won't hurt you, girl," he said, talking to Charlotte softly. "I promise to be as careful as I possibly can." He looked up at the dog's owner. It occurred to him that he didn't know her name, but getting acquainted could wait until later. This was more important. "I'm afraid that I'm going to have to put Charlotte under."

She looked at him with concern. "Do you have to?"

"I'm afraid that she isn't going to let me do what I have to do to her if she's awake," Sam told her. "Charlotte is not going to sit still for a scalpel or a needle piercing her skin when I go to sew her up. The noises that she'll make are guaranteed to break your heart. There is no way that I can do what I have to do when Charlotte is carrying on and crying during the process."

Charlotte's owner nodded, and then she shrugged. "Okay, Doctor, do what you have to do."

"I will," he answered. "And if you will please sit out in the lobby, I can get started."

"If you don't mind, Doctor, I'd rather stay here with you in case you need anything," the woman said, "or if you need any assistance."

"That won't be necessary," he told her. "I don't have an assistant when I operate."

"Maybe you should." She knew she was speaking out of turn, but Charlotte was very precious to her, and she had the impression that the vet was tired when she had roused him out of bed. She was amazed that he had managed to throw some clothes on before he opened his door. "I do have some training when it comes to this sort of surgery. I just prefer someone else taking the lead if it turns out to be complicated," she told him. "The second you feel that I'm getting in the way, just say the word, and I will back off, I promise." She looked at him intently, as if willing him to give a positive answer. "Okay?"

He was ready to turn her down flat. But the truth of it was that he felt that he really did need help in this situation. And although these were actually pretty dire conditions, this would most likely be the best way to test the woman's mettle.

"Okay," he told her, then nodded toward the sink in the corner. "Wash up."

She smiled hugely, then took in a deep breath and went to comply.

"By the way," Sam called after her, thinking he was going to need to be able to call her something as they got to work, "what's your name?"

"I didn't tell you?" she asked. In all the excitement, she must have forgotten, she thought.

"No, you didn't."

"It's Gina."

He nodded. "Nice to meet you, Gina. Let's get to work."

"Yes, Doctor."

He caught himself thinking that had a nice ring to it.

Chapter Four

Sam realized almost immediately that there was more damage done to the miniature collie than was noticeable at first glance. But now that he had Charlotte on the operating table with all the lights shining on the wounded animal, Sam could see that the rampaging pit bull had done a great deal more damage to his victim than he had thought at first.

He had sedated his patient, but even so, he still approached her very cautiously. If Charlotte was even partially conscious, he didn't want to risk frightening her.

"Would you happen to know who this pit bull belonged to?" he asked his unofficial assistant. Gina was right by his side, and she appeared to be nervously observing him as well as her pet.

"A neighbor, I think," Gina answered. She looked at him, clearly worried that something was off. "Why are you asking?"

"A dog that does this much damage to another living creature without being provoked is clearly dangerous. That dog shouldn't be walking around without being restrained," Sam said in all sincerity. "Your dog didn't do anything to provoke the pit bull, did she?"

"No!" Gina denied with feeling. "All Charlotte did was look up at the pit bull, nothing more. I doubt if he really even had time to register her presence. He just came charging around the corner, barking and growling and clearly ready to turn her into a doggie version of fast food." Gina looked down at her pet on the operating table. Her heart was clearly hurting for her poor dog. "I was barely able to get the animal to run off before Charlotte became a pincushion."

Gina was sorely tempted to run her hand along her pet's fur, desperately wanting to comfort the miniature collie. But even though the dog had been sedated, she was afraid that the contact might rouse Charlotte, and then anything the veterinarian was attempting to accomplish would be summarily destroyed or, at the very least, put on hold.

"It's all right," Sam told her. "You can touch her."

Gina looked up at him in surprise. "Do you practice mind reading, too?"

He laughed softly. "No need for mind reading. Remember, I have a pet dog, too. It's not so hard to guess what you're thinking. I would be thinking the same thing if all this was new to me, and I wasn't a veterinarian."

Gina gazed down at her sedated collie. She shivered a little. "When I think of what might have happened..." Her voice faded away. Tears gathered in her eyes.

"You can't dwell on what might have been," Sam said. "You need to focus on the fact that you managed to save your pet, and you ran that aggressive dog off before he could rip Charlotte into tiny pieces." It was time for him to get to work. "All right, are you sure you're up to being in the same room with your pet while I operate?" he asked Gina. "I won't think any less of you if you decide you'd rather take refuge in the waiting area."

But Gina was adamant as she shook her head. "No, I will be fine. I want to be able to help."

"All right, you can stay. After you wash your hands, put on a pair of surgical gloves. You'll find the gloves on that shelf," he directed, nodding his head toward a cabinet against the wall.

Gina followed his instructions, going over toward the sink and washing her hands. Once they were washed, she dried them, then slipped on a pair of surgical gloves.

Sam saw a hint of a frown on her lips. "Is something wrong?"

"Well, they're a little large," she told the veterinarian.

"I wasn't really planning on having an assistant, even though I was turning that idea over in my mind," Sam admitted. "That's why I didn't have a lot of sizes available."

"Hey, I'm not complaining," she said. "You just asked, and I believe in always being honest."

He smiled at her. "Well, that's a really good trait to have."

At that moment, Sam's own dog was whining and circled around the room. Up to this point, Rocky had been behaving so well, Sam had almost forgotten about her. But even so, he knew that he couldn't risk having the German shepherd in the room while he operated on another animal. Rocky might make a sudden move that could really throw everything off.

"Okay, Rocky, my girl," Sam said. "It's time for you to go and stand guard at the door to the clinic."

Rocky obligingly trotted off to the clinic's front door and assumed a guard position.

Gina's mouth all but dropped open. "She understood you," she cried in surprise.

"Dogs understand more than we give them credit for. It just takes a great deal of practice," Sam told Gina with an easy smile.

Gina laughed under her breath and shook her head in amazement. "You know, I'm beginning to think that you're right."

"Of course I'm right. I'm the veterinarian," he pointed out with a grin. "Do you doubt me?"

Gina began to feel hopeful. She was glad she had come to Sam's clinic, even if it was an ungodly hour. "Heaven forbid."

"Good answer," he said. Then, looking at her, he asked, "Are you ready?"

Gina pulled her shoulders back. "I'm ready." She

looked grateful that he hadn't read her the riot act for waking him up in the middle of the night. But her actions were warranted. And he was just doing what a dedicated veterinarian should. Gina came over to the table and stood next to him. "All right, tell me what to do and I'll do it."

"It's simple," he told her. "Just be there to keep her calm and make sure she doesn't suddenly wake up and attempt to bolt off the operating table."

Her eyes widened. "Has that ever happened to you?"

"No, not yet," he answered. "But that doesn't mean that there can't be a first time. How long have you had her?" he asked as he prepared to operate.

Gina didn't even have to pause to think. "I've had Charlotte since she was a puppy. Three years," she specified.

Sam nodded. "So she'll definitely respond to the sound of your voice when she wakes up."

Gina took a deep breath and nodded, never taking her eyes off her pet. She appeared to have braced herself. "Okay, let's do this."

As he began the surgery, Sam expected to hear Gina moan, or at the very least, give some indication that the procedure disturbed her. But to Sam's surprise, his "assistant" remained completely stoic, silently observing as he methodically repaired the damage that the pit bull had done to what appeared to be an exceedingly mild-mannered, easygoing pet.

"How are you doing?" Sam felt compelled to ask

his impromptu assistant when he was partially through the procedure. He noted that Gina had never taken her eyes off her pet while he operated.

"I'm fine," she answered, watching the collie's face. And then, as if she felt compelled to ask, "Is it going to be much longer?"

"Why? Do you want to take a break?" He was about to tell her she should go sit down and rest.

But Gina surprised him by answering, "No, I'm just afraid that Charlotte might suddenly wake up and realize what is going on."

Sam shook his head. "Trust me, she has enough anesthesia in her to keep her out for a long while. She's not in any danger of suddenly waking up."

"Then I'm fine," she assured him. "I just wish she could feel me petting her."

Sam smiled at the woman's concern. "Somehow, she feels it."

"You sound awfully sure of yourself," Gina whispered, as if she could use a little more reinforcement.

"I am," he told her. But he could sense that she wanted more reassurance. As he carefully stitched up the dog, he added, "It's a gut feeling. It's something you learn after a while from working with pets. Trust me."

"I do," she told him in all sincerity.

He spared her a quick look before turning his eyes back to his work. But although he had hardly known Gina for more than just a few minutes, Sam believed she meant what she said. He flashed her a smile. "It won't be too much longer," he promised her.

"Take as long as you need," she told him. "I'm not going anywhere and neither is Charlotte."

Sam laughed. "I kind of figured that part out."

Gina kept her eyes glued to every movement he made.

Sam tried his best to finish up without rushing through the procedure. That wasn't his way, but then, neither was having an assistant at his side. Not that he hadn't thought about it more than once, but it had been just a pipe dream more than anything else.

This wasn't bad, he caught himself thinking.

Sam carefully coached himself through what he was doing. Finally, the last stitch was placed, and he cut the thread. "Done," he announced to Gina.

"You're really finished?" Gina asked him.

"I'm finished," Sam confirmed. "You can stand down."

"I don't need to stand down," she told him, but even as she said it, her legs felt almost watery. "But would you mind if I sat down?"

Sam gestured toward a stool in the corner. "Please do."

She all but collapsed onto it, releasing a huge breath.

"Tired?" Sam asked her, somewhat concerned. She was obviously emotionally invested in her pet's surgery and had been out super late walking her dog.

Gina was about to deny it, then decided there was no point. She wasn't trying to project a superhuman image. Besides, now that the surgery was over, she was suddenly exhausted. "You have no idea," she told him.

Sam grinned at the pretty young woman. He could sense just what she had to be experiencing. He had been there himself a number of times with his own pet. "Oh, yes, I do," he assured her.

Chapter Five

"I don't think it's a good idea for you to be driving home at this hour and in this sleepy condition—wherever home might be," Sam qualified.

He had taken down Gina's contact information, but she wasn't surprised he hadn't committed it to memory. He'd been completely caught up in her miniature collie's condition. "I have a spare bedroom where you can sack out," he told her. "Or, if you would prefer, you can catch a nap on one of my sofas. Whatever your preference is will be just fine with me."

But Gina shook her head. "I couldn't do that," she protested. She didn't like imposing on the veterinarian any more than she already had.

"Why can't you?"

"It just wouldn't be right," Gina insisted, feeling somewhat uncomfortable.

Sam shook his head as if completely lost. "According to whom?"

"Well, for one thing, I don't even know you," Gina pointed out.

It clearly took effort for Sam not to laugh. "I'm the man you got out of bed in the middle of the night in order to save your miniature collie—and I did," he concluded. "What more do you need to know?"

Gina frowned. "When you say it like that, I guess what I said does sound a little silly," she admitted.

Sam smiled and nodded as if satisfied. "All right, then we're in agreement."

"I didn't say that," Gina objected. He was putting words into her mouth, she thought.

"Why don't you take a cue from your pet and just sleep?" Sam suggested. "Trust me, you are going to need your strength when Charlotte wakes up."

Gina had a feeling that the veterinarian knew exactly what he was talking about. She decided to stop fighting him. "Is your sofa out of the way, Dr. Sterling?" she asked.

Sam glanced at his watch. "It's six thirty in the morning. The way I see it, *everything* is out of the way at this hour." He beckoned for the collie's owner to follow him. "The sofa is over here." Something seemed to suddenly occur to him. "Is there anyone you want to call to let them know you and Charlotte are here and safe?" he asked.

The fact that he thought of asking struck her as exceedingly thoughtful. Gina shook her head. "No, nobody local. Besides, I don't intend to sleep very long—if, very honestly, at all," she added.

Sam seemed to bite his tongue. "Sleep as long as

you need to. There is no hurry on my end." He produced a blanket and a pillow for her and set them on the sofa. "Here you go."

She almost told him she didn't need either, but she had to admit that this was all rather nice of him, and the early hour still felt rather chilly. So, taking the pillow and blanket, she told him, "Thank you." Making herself comfortable, Gina spread out the blanket and then curled up beneath it, tucking the pillow under her head. "I won't be long," she repeated.

Sam flashed her a quick smile. "Don't worry—I don't charge by the hour," he assured her.

"I just thought you'd want to know that I would be clearing out soon," she said.

"Duly noted. But I honestly wasn't worried," Sam added as he walked out of the room.

Despite the fact that he'd left the overhead lights on, Gina felt her eyelids grow heavy and found herself struggling to keep them open.

Gina couldn't say when she had closed her eyes; she just knew that she must have. Eyes flying open, she sat up, roused into wakefulness by the tempting scent of toast, eggs and bacon. Her stomach practically growled in response, and she could feel her mouth watering. She couldn't remember having had that response to food in a long time. She really didn't think she was that hungry, but obviously, she was wrong.

It took her a few moments to orient herself, unaccustomed to falling asleep in unfamiliar places. She looked around for Charlotte before she remembered that her miniature collie would still be asleep in the cage that the veterinarian had carefully placed her in.

Blinking the sleep out of her eyes, and not knowing her way around, Gina followed her nose to the source of the tempting smell. She found Dr. Sterling standing by a stove, cooking. He lifted a frying pan off the stovetop and divided the pan's contents between two plates, then placed the pan back on a cool burner.

"You can cook?" Gina asked, stunned.

She had startled him, but he managed not to miss a beat as he turned around to look at her. "Certainly looks that way," he responded. "Why do you sound so surprised?"

She shrugged and walked into the room. "I just thought that being a veterinarian was enough of an accomplishment," she told him. "Being able to cook seems like overkill, in my estimation."

"Are you telling me you don't think that guys can cook?" he asked as he picked up the plates and brought them over to the small kitchen table. "I didn't think you would be guilty of stereotyping," he said.

"It's not that," she protested, then realized that she *was* guilty of that. "Well, maybe it is. Most of the guys I know literally cannot boil water."

"Well, if my brothers and I were guilty of being

unable to boil water, we would have probably wound up starving to death," Sam told her. He took a bottle of ketchup out of the refrigerator and placed it on the table between their plates. "My father worked really hard to build up his company so he could provide for us," he told her.

Gina caught her lip between her teeth but knew it would be impolite to ask the obvious question.

"My mother died when I was a kid," he said, volunteering the information. "There were five of us kids in the family, all boys. I was the oldest. My father hired a live-in nanny to watch over us, but just to play it safe, he also wanted all of us to know how to cook in case the nanny didn't turn out. He didn't want to have a bunch of helpless boys on his hands," Sam clarified.

Gina smiled at him. "Your father sounds like he was a very wise man."

"He was. Still is," Sam added with pride.

She felt herself turning red. "I guess I'm not wording this right. I didn't mean to imply that he was no longer among the living."

"I know. I just wanted to make things clear," Sam said. "I didn't mean to embarrass you. I guess that's the disadvantage of growing up without a mother, not knowing how to behave around women. Although I have to say that Randi did try her best."

"Randi?" Gina questioned, a little bit confused.

"The nanny that my dad hired to raise us after our mother died," Sam explained.

"Is Randi still around?" Gina asked, guessing that the nanny was the one who had taught the brothers the basic elements of how to cook.

Sam grinned fondly. "Oh, she's very much around. I don't think we could get her to run off if we wanted to—not that we would want to. She used to come by every Sunday to check in on us, but she hasn't been over for a while."

"Why every Sunday?" she asked, thinking that sounded rather unusual.

"Sundays are when we gather at my dad's house," he explained. "He's still living in the same house where we all grew up. I really don't think Dad can bring himself to get rid of it. As he likes to say, that was where he was happiest and where he built up all his precious memories." A fond smile curved the veterinarian's lips. "I suppose the same thing goes for the rest of us," he told her. "We all have our own places at this point, but the house where my father lives will always be thought of as 'home' to us."

Sam looked up at her and laughed at whatever expression must have been on her face. "I guess you got more of an answer than you bargained for. Sorry if I overwhelmed you. I don't usually talk this much."

"I'm not overwhelmed," she told him. "If anything, I'm flattered you shared all of this with me. It sounds as if you have an extremely nice family."

"I guess you could say that," Sam agreed with a warm smile. "Although there were times when all I really wanted to do was just string them all up, or at the very least, strangle them."

She gave him a disbelieving look. "You don't really mean that."

"Oh, yeah, I do," he contradicted. "Don't forget, I was the oldest one, which meant that at times I had to watch them. That cut into any free time I had."

Why would he have had to watch them? she wondered. "But you said you had a live-in nanny who was there to watch over you."

He laughed, remembering. "Randi was never a pushover. She was kind, but she was strict, and she had rules she wanted us to follow. And since I was the oldest, I was in charge of the others. It was my job to make sure that they were all well-behaved."

"I never thought of it that way," she admitted.

"Well, in your defense, most people don't," Sam told her. "They think that having five brothers in a family is all fun and games, like an episode from some sitcom." He laughed to himself. "Actually, it's really far from that at times. I have to admit that if any of us were threatened, we were immediately there for one another. But if it was a different sort of situation, you know, something internal, we were there at each other's throats. At least when we were kids."

"And now?" Gina asked him, curious.

"We're so busy with our separate careers," he told her honestly, "we don't have time."

"But you do get together every Sunday," she said, just to stay clear.

He nodded. "It's more for our father than for us," he explained. "And it's also to pay homage to our mother—which in its own way is also for our father. Our mother loved Sunday dinners."

"You sound like you're a very close family," she told him enviously.

He smiled at her. "Well, looking back at it now, I guess that you are right. Although I have to admit that there were times we would wind up squabbling with one another over dinner. But between my dad and Randi, they managed to get us to all behave."

Just then, her collie whined. Sam was on his feet instantly. "Sounds like Charlotte is awake," he said, heading for the clinic where the miniature collie was recovering in a cage.

Gina was right behind him.

Chapter Six

Charlotte was standing in her cage, her sad little face pressed against the bars. The moment Gina came into the room, the miniature collie began to whine and cry pathetically, as if her mistress had come to break her out of jail and erase all the pain.

Seeing her like that, Gina's heart almost broke. She dropped to her knees and reached into the cage as far as she could. Charlotte curled into her hand so she could be petted.

Gina glanced up at the veterinarian. She knew the protocol when it came to dealing with pets after they'd had surgery, but if Sam had any special idiosyncrasies when it came to that, she wanted to make sure she took them into account. She didn't want to break any of the veterinarian's rules. Sam had done her a huge favor, taking care of her dog as well as allowing her to crash on his sofa. Making her breakfast was just a bonus on top of that. She definitely wouldn't want to insult him by stepping on his toes.

"It is all right for me to pet Charlotte, isn't it?" Gina asked. She worded it so that she sounded hopeful rather than just assuming she was in the right. "I'm not breaking any of the rules, am I?"

"As long as you don't pet Charlotte too hard—but I think you already know that, right?" Sam asked with a wide smile.

"Yes. I'd like to take the poor thing into my arms and just squeeze her as hard as I can, but don't worry—I'm not about to do that," she said quickly.

Sam nodded, no doubt familiar with that urge when it came to recuperating pets. "The time you can do that safely will come," he promised her. "Just remind yourself that all this restraint is for Charlotte's own good, and she'll be up and on her feet soon enough. You just have to allow her to heal first, and she'll be better than new."

"I know. I've just never been the patient type when it comes to waiting for something I had my heart set on. I was always good about waiting when it came to something someone else needed." Gina took a deep breath. "That being said, when can I take Charlotte home?"

Sam laughed softly. He knew he would have been disappointed if she hadn't asked that. "Probably later on today. It all depends on how quickly Charlotte recovers and bounces back." He added, "I can give you a call, and you can come by later and pick Charlotte up if you like."

But that approach didn't really sit well with Gina, and she shook her head. "If you don't mind, I'd like to hang around here until I can take my little girl home with me."

"Why? Don't trust me?" he asked with a smile.

"Oh, it's not that," Gina said, quickly shooting down that accusation. "I'd just like to be around in case you might need me for something." Thinking, she added, "If you have any chores or anything you'd like taken care of, just let me know, and I'll do it."

Sam looked at her as if caught off guard by her suggestion. But he seemed to give it some honest thought, then asked, "Do you really mean that?"

"Yes," she said with feeling. "I wouldn't have said it if I didn't. The one thing you should know about me is that I never say things I don't mean. Ever."

And if she was going to remain here, waiting for Charlotte to be well enough so she could take her home, Gina decided she might as well be useful. As a matter of fact, she could think of it as an audition. She really did want to be the man's assistant, at the least in a part-time capacity. Besides, she had never done well sitting still. Immobility made her feel antsy, although she was not about to tell Sam that.

"You're not even tempted to stretch the truth just a little?" he asked.

Gina shook her head. "Not even a little bit," she told him. "If a person lies once, they're inclined to lie again and again. The second and third times are far easier than the first. It becomes a trap that's hard to get out of, and I'd rather not slide into it to begin with."

Sam studied her for a moment, and then he smiled. "Were you ever a Girl Scout when you were growing up?"

"As a matter of fact, I was," she said, surprised. "My cousin Alice wanted to be a Girl Scout, but she was shy and didn't want to join alone. My mother prevailed upon my better instincts, and I wound up joining with Alice." She smiled, remembering. "I had a great time with her."

"I knew it," he declared. "You have that Girl Scout aura about you."

She wasn't sure exactly how to take that. Was the man making fun of her, or was he just paying her an offhand compliment? But either way, he had gotten out of bed in the middle of the night and operated on Charlotte without complaint, so she could cut him some slack. Actually, she could cut him a lot of slack.

"Well, now that I think of it, there are several things you could do for me if you're actually serious about wanting to do something while you're here," Sam told her, watching her face carefully.

"Great," Gina responded in all seriousness. "Like what?" She hoped she hadn't opened herself up to doing something she might wind up regretting.

"This probably is going to sound a little archaic to someone as tech-savvy as you undoubtedly are, but I need to have my patient files organized according to name and procedure. Since I'm the only one holding down the fort ever since I opened up this 'fort,' things have kind of gotten away from me over the years."

He paused, as if expecting Gina to laugh at him. When she didn't, he continued, "If you don't think of me as being too lax, I'll gather the files together for you so you can help me catch up."

"The only thing you need to do is give me your paper files, show me where your computer is and then just get out of my way," she told him. "I'll take care of the rest. And whatever I don't manage to get to today, I promise I'll come back tomorrow and finish the job then."

He looked about to agree, but then something seemed to occur to him. "Don't you have a job you have to go to?" Sam asked.

"I'm afraid that right now I'm in between jobs," Gina told him. "I do have just enough put aside—I think—to pay you for Charlotte's surgery. If it turns out that I don't, I can make arrangements to pay you off over time—with interest." She had no intention of taking advantage of him. "I'm not planning on skipping out on what I owe you," she told him in all seriousness.

Sam laughed. "I wasn't really worried about you not paying the bill," he said. "Getting back to my original request, do you think you can do it? Can you organize those files I mentioned?"

"No problem. I can do it in my sleep," she told him, adding, "with my eyes closed."

"Well, if I had my preferences, I'd rather that you were awake and your eyes were open," Sam told her.

Gina did her best not to grin as she shook her head. "Picky, picky, picky. I guess I can meet your conditions," she told him with a laugh. "Okay, just give me those paper files of your patients, tell me how you want the end result to look and then just let me get to it."

Sam marveled at how simple she made it all sound. He had to admit that he liked her approach.

"With pleasure," Sam told her sincerely. "And I'll look in on our patient—in between the others that will be arriving. By the way, there's a coffeepot brewing in the front office, if you're interested. And there's some creamer in a small refrigerator, if you need it."

Gina took her coffee black when she wanted to stay awake, but she nodded. "Duly noted." She glanced down at Charlotte. "Mama's going to be working in the other room, sweetie. I'll check in on you from time to time to make sure you're doing all right," she told the miniature collie, leaning in and running her hand over her head.

Gina caught Sam looking at her. He seemed amused, she thought. "What?" she asked. "Why are you grinning like that?"

"Do you always talk to your dog like that?" Sam asked.

She didn't quite follow him. "Like what?"

"Like Charlotte was your child and could understand what you were saying to her," Sam answered.

She didn't understand the confusion. "Of course she can understand. I believe all animals can understand what we say to them. Don't you?"

On some level, Sam had always believed that, but most of the people he dealt with, including pet owners, didn't buy into that, at least not wholeheartedly.

Sam smiled at her. "Really?"

"Of course really," Gina answered.

"Glad to hear that," he said. He glanced at his watch. "My first patient is coming in at eight. The pet's owner has to be at work early and wanted to drop off his pet before then." He often did things like that, which was what put him in such demand with his clients.

Gina nodded. "I'll make myself scarce before they come in."

He went to get the stack of files he had compiled but never seemed to get to, then handed them to her. "Why would you want to make yourself scarce?" he asked.

She looked at him, slightly confused. "Don't you want me to? I mean, I'm not exactly working for you."

"No," he agreed, "you don't. But you did mention that you might want to."

She looked at him, not sure if this was going where

she hoped it would. "Yes, I did..." She trailed off, waiting for him to complete his thought.

"If you're still interested in becoming my assistant, why don't we say that this could be a trial run?" he suggested. "If you still want to work for me by the time you finish organizing those files, I'll hire you."

Gina grinned widely at him. "That sounds really good to me." Just then, the doorbell to the clinic rang. "I believe that's your patient showing up early."

"Do you want to get that for me?" he asked. Was he curious to see how she would act?

"Consider it done," she told him. It didn't even occur to Gina to feel nervous, even though she didn't know who was standing on the other side of the door. She was eager to get started working as his assistant.

Chapter Seven

Sean Sterling was about to start talking the moment that the clinic's front door opened. But he suddenly found himself at a loss for words other than "Hello." He gave the young woman who opened the door a long, appreciative look up and down. The curvy, sexy blonde was gorgeous, no two ways about it.

Realizing that he needed to follow up his greeting with something that conveyed that he was capable of reasonable thought, he asked, "Um, is Sam around?" He peered into the clinic.

"Do you mean Dr. Sterling?" the blonde asked.

Sean laughed under his breath. It was difficult to think of his oldest brother in terms of being a doctor of any sort. As far as he was concerned, the veterinarian the woman referred to was just "Sammy," the brother who had taken care of him and Sebastian when their mother was no longer there.

And now, Sean thought, smiling to himself, his extremely dedicated bachelor brother seemed to have found someone for himself. Or at least it looked that way.

But before he allowed himself to jump to any conclusions, Sean decided to explore the young woman's rather unique wording. A person who was romantically involved with someone did not usually refer to that person by their official title.

"Okay, let's go with that," Sean agreed loftily. "Is *Dr.* Sterling around?" Man, it was really difficult getting those words out without laughing, Sean thought, doing his best to keep the corners of his mouth from curving.

"He is, but he's busy right now," the woman told him, running interference for the veterinarian. In her opinion, the man looked a great deal like Sam, but maybe they weren't actually related. "Is there anything that I can help you with?" Maybe he had a pet in his car.

Sean was going to have to take his big brother aside for a talk. This very probably could be an entirely new development that his brother didn't know how to handle. To the best of Sean's recollection, Sam had never had anyone in his life he had ever referred to as a girlfriend, not in any permanent sense. Or even in a fleeting one, Sean thought.

"All right, I have a question for you," Sean said, taking a new approach. "Have you been with Sam long? In a working capacity, I mean."

"Are you asking me how long I've been working as his assistant?" the blonde asked, doing her best to attempt to clear things up. Now that she thought about it, she could see how the man she was talking to might have made that mistake.

Sean nodded. "I guess that's what I'm doing," he said. He found himself utterly fascinated by the woman.

"I'm not his assistant," she informed him.

"Then what are you doing here?" Sean asked, his voice trailing off.

"Being helpful," she answered. "I'm guilty of waking him up in the middle of the night—"

"Oh?" This sounded even better than he had thought. He might have been grinning too hard.

"A pit bull attacked my dog while I was walking her early this morning. Someone had given me Dr. Sterling's name, saying he was an excellent pet surgeon. My poor Charlotte was in a really bad way and bleeding. I'm new here. I didn't know what else to do or where else to go, so I drove over here and knocked on Dr. Sterling's door even though I knew he had to be asleep at that hour. But rather than read me the riot act for waking him up, he immediately got out of bed and agreed to sew up Charlotte."

"That sounds like Sam," Sean agreed, nodding his head. "All heart and ready to jump in and save a pet, no matter if it's night or day."

The woman looked impressed. "You sound as if you know him well."

"As well as one brother can know another," Sean replied.

She nodded her head. "I thought you looked like him."

"Now, I've been nothing but polite to you," Sean told her, pretending to pout. "There's no reason for you to insult me." And then he smiled. "I'm sorry—I didn't catch your name."

"I didn't throw it," she answered innocently.

"No, I guess you didn't," he agreed with a quiet chuckle. And then he asked her point-blank, "What is your name?"

"It's Gina," she told him.

"Gina," he repeated. "I'm Sean. Sean Sterling."

Just then, Sam walked in and headed directly toward Sean. "I thought that was your voice I heard," he said to his youngest brother. "Are you in here harassing my patient's owner?"

"You know me. I'm just getting acquainted," Sean told him.

"Yeah, I'll bet. What are you doing here, really?" Sam pressed, giving him a penetrating look.

"Oddly enough," Sean said, "Dad sent me." He turned his head toward Gina. "We start work early in the construction business."

Sam ignored that and instead asked, "And just why did Dad send you?"

"He just wanted to see how you were doing. Said something about not having heard from you in a while. This is the distinct disadvantage of working with your father," Sean told Gina. "I hadn't thought about that complication."

Sam glanced at Gina and explained, "My dad."

"He means 'our' dad," Sean interjected.

Sam rolled his eyes. "*Our* dad," he corrected, "started his own company out here years ago."

"What does your father do?" Gina asked attentively.

"He's in construction. As a matter of fact, he built this development," Sam said as an aside, then continued, "Sean eventually horned his way into the company and refused to take no for an answer no matter how hard our dad tried to talk him out of it."

Sean raised his chin. "Our dad knew a good thing when he saw it."

"Which brings us to today," Sam said conclusively, "and what you're doing here." He gave his youngest brother a look.

"I already told you," Sean insisted. "Dad wanted me to check in on you because he said that he hadn't heard from you."

Sam frowned. "The man saw me at dinner last Sunday."

"I mean besides that," Sean said pointedly, "and you know it. Sunday dinner doesn't mean anything—unless you miss it."

Sam laughed, shaking his head. "Does that man have any idea how many fathers don't see their sons for weeks at a time? Months? Sometimes even years?"

"He knows," Sean agreed, "but that's not how our

father raised us. Nor would he deign to put up with it," he added matter-of-factly.

The expression on Sam's face was less than happy. Gina must have noticed. "You don't know how lucky you are," she told Sam. "A lot of people don't have family in their lives, or if they do, they don't know where they are."

"I take it that you belong to that group," Sean guessed.

"My parents are both dead," she told them, though it seemed to still hurt. "I have a sister, but she doesn't stay in touch except when she needs money. Then I get a letter. Once I answer it and send her some money, that's it for communication for a long time. Unless she needs more money." And then she smiled as she looked at her pet. "That's why I guess I'm so attached to Charlotte here." Gina nodded toward the dog in the cage. "She doesn't ask for anything except to be petted and loved."

Sean chuckled, smiling at Gina. "My kind of dog."

Sam frowned at him. "Down, boy," he ordered.

Sean pulled his shoulders back and pretended to salute. "Yes, sir. Well, now that I see you're in one piece and have a perfectly logical reason for not getting in touch with Dad, I will get out of your hair. But call him," he urged. "First chance you get. It'll make Dad happy, and it'll keep him from complaining." Sean grinned. "I guess he's going to need to get another hobby."

"The man's in construction," Gina said. "How much more of a hobby does your father need?"

Sean laughed under his breath. "You'd be surprised."

"You said there were five of you?" Gina asked.

"That's right," Sam answered. "Five brothers, separated by a year to a year and a half."

She paused as if trying to imagine what that was like. "Your father's a very lucky man," she told the two brothers enviously.

Sam fixed her with a look as if intrigued. "You want to tell him that?"

"Now, there's an idea," Sean said, turning it over in his mind.

"What is?" Sam asked, evidently not following Sean's trail of thought.

"Why don't you invite Gina to dinner this Sunday?" Sean asked Sam, nodding at her.

Gina blinked, no doubt completely lost. "Excuse me?" she asked, certain that she had misunderstood what Sam's brother had just said. How had he gotten from point A to point B like that without even blinking?

"My brother seems to be tongue-tied," Sean said. "How would you like to come to dinner this Sunday? I'm sure my father would welcome a pretty face at the table. Heaven knows the rest of us would."

"You're getting ahead of yourself, Sean," Sam told him.

"That's because you can't seem to get ahead at all," Sean said, looking at his brother pointedly.

Gina, meanwhile, was apparently still deciding just what her answer to the invitation was going to be.

Chapter Eight

"Um, Sam, could I have a word with you?" Sean asked, nodding toward the clinic's door.

Sam looked at his brother, somewhat bewildered. "Sure," he answered and waited for Sean to continue. After all, his baby brother had never had a problem talking before. Of all of them, Sean was probably the most vocal, never keeping his thoughts to himself if he felt like voicing them out loud. It was no wonder that Sean was the one who was finally able to talk their father into hiring him, even when Sanford Sterling had been dead set against bringing any of his sons into a business that the man felt was beneath them. That was not the reason, he had claimed, that he had sent them all off to college.

But Sean had other thoughts on the matter and had made them known. The rest of the family always maintained that Sean could talk the wings off an angel in flight if he set his mind to it.

Sean glanced toward the woman standing with them in the clinic, his implication clear. Still, he stressed, "Alone."

To the best of Sam's knowledge, Sean was never shy about any topic, but for the sake of moving this along, he shrugged. "Sure." To Gina, Sam added, "If you'll excuse us, I'll be right back."

"No problem," Gina told him and moved back to organizing the patient files. "I'll be right here," she promised, already sounding preoccupied.

As if satisfied that he had his brother's attention, Sean walked into an adjacent room, then turned to face Sam. "Is she working for you?" Sean asked.

Sam was caught off guard. That was a strange question for Sean to ask. "No." But he paused when he saw the skeptical look come over Sean's face. He supposed that his youngest brother had seen what Gina was doing and figured she had to be working for the clinic. "It's complicated," Sam amended.

"I've got time. *Un*complicate things for me," Sean encouraged him.

Sam sighed. He wasn't going to find any peace until he spelled it all out for Sean. Clearly. "I operated on her miniature collie first thing this morning and told her to come back later today to pick up her pet. But Gina wanted to hang around to watch over her dog. She told me that while she hung around, she wanted to be useful. To her, that means actually *doing* something. She asked me if there was anything I needed to have taken care of. Since I don't have an assistant," Sam said, deliberately avoiding Sean's eyes, "I've let my files pile up. Gina volunteered to put them in order while she waited until she could take her dog home."

"In lieu of payment?" Sean guessed.

"No," Sam answered with feeling. "She didn't even try to barter. She said she definitely intends to pay me for her collie's surgery. She said that she just hated sitting around, doing nothing."

"Sam," Sean said, duly impressed, "you need to snatch this woman up—for more reasons than one." He pinned Sam with a look. "Didn't you tell me—more than once, I might add—that you were thinking about hiring an assistant?"

"Yes, but I wasn't talking about right this minute," Sam maintained.

Sean rolled his eyes. "If not now, then when? Just before you die?"

Sam frowned, annoyed. "No. I just don't like being rushed."

Sean made a face, letting Sam know he wasn't buying any of this. "Sam, you've been talking about getting an assistant for five years now. Trust me, it's way past the 'rushing' point. Hire her," he stressed. "You know I'm right."

"What I know is that you're a giant pain in the neck," Sam told his brother.

"That's beside the point," Sean said dismissively. "But if I wasn't, you'd never do anything. Someone needs to light a fire under you to get you moving for your own good, big brother," he pointed out. "Now hire the woman. You can always fire her later on if you feel things aren't working out."

Sam's frown deepened even more. "Easy for you to say."

Sean gave him an innocent look. "You want me to hire her for you? Then, like I said, if it doesn't work out, I can always fire her for you. You won't have to do a thing except grunt," Sean said brightly. "Does that suit you?"

"I can do my own hiring and firing, thank you," Sam told him. What a giant pain Sean was. "And my own grunting, too."

"Good," Sean said with finality. "Then stop talking about it and dragging your feet and just do it." He placed an encouraging hand on Sam's shoulder, as if silently urging him to take the proper steps. He went on, "When I was growing up, I always looked up to you. Don't give me a reason to change my mind now, Sammy."

Sam closed his eyes. In his heart, he knew Sean was right. He just didn't like being bullied into things. "All right, all right, all right," Sam declared, coming very close to losing his temper.

"So you'll hire her?" Sean asked, keeping his eyes all but glued on Sam's face.

"Yes," Sam almost snapped. "I'll hire her if it gets you to back off and shut up."

Rather than say anything else, Sean pantomimed sealing and locking his lips.

For his trouble, Sam hit Sean in the shoulder with the flat of his hand. "I didn't mean for you to go utterly quiet."

Sean merely smiled widely in response.

"You can talk, Sean. I don't want you falling to the ground, gasping for air," Sam told him. Seeing that he wasn't really making any impression on his brother, Sam said, "Let's go back into the other room. I don't want Gina to think we just deserted her and left her high and dry."

Sean, meanwhile, smiled at his brother's words. This did sound promising. Whether he realized it or not, Sam had just indicated that he cared what the woman thought. While Sam was never outright impolite, he never acted as if he actually cared what a woman thought of his behavior. What his brother had just said gave him a measure of hope.

"By all means," Sean said, turning on his heel to go back to the main room of the clinic, "let's get back to the woman before she decides that we've deserted her and just leaves."

But Sam knew Gina was not about to go anywhere. "She wouldn't leave without Charlotte, and she's not taking the dog until I give her the go-ahead to do so," he emphasized. He was very sure about that.

Sean didn't bother hiding his grin. "How does it feel being king of your own little empire, Sammy?"

Sam didn't answer other than to wave his hand dismissively at his youngest brother. As he made his way back into the clinic, closely followed by Sean, he dreaded inviting her to dinner in front of Sean, but if he didn't say anything, Sean would beat him to it. He really didn't want this turning into any sort of verbal competition. If Gina did agree to attend Sunday dinner, he wanted her coming as his guest, not Sean's.

In his opinion, Gina had looked really hungry to attend a family event. He just felt it was something he could do for her. Never mind that she had dragged him out of a dead sleep early this morning. He'd untangle the details of his reasoning later on.

"Gina," Sam said as he walked into the clinic.

Lost in paperwork, Gina looked up belatedly. "Yes?" she questioned hopefully. No doubt she was wondering if Charlotte had recovered and if she could take her beloved miniature collie home.

"Are you free this Sunday at three o'clock?" Sam asked her. For the first time in his life, he felt as if he was tripping over his own tongue.

She blinked as if confused by his question. "Excuse me, Dr. Sterling?"

"What my somewhat socially awkward big brother is trying to find out is if you are free this Sunday to come over to the house for Sunday dinner," Sean said.

Sam silently upbraided his brother in his mind. He didn't need Sean speaking for him. "You understand that there's no pressure for you to attend," he told Gina, uttering the words through clenched teeth as he gave Sean a dirty look.

"I'm confused," Gina told him. "Are you asking me to come, or is this your veiled way of telling me you *don't* want me to come?"

"My brother has never been suave. Smart," Sean told her with feeling, "but not suave. He's inviting you to dinner. With all of us," he emphasized.

"How many are there in 'all of us'?" Gina asked curiously.

"Five, plus our dad," Sean told her.

"And you all show up?" she asked, clearly surprised.

"Absolutely. Under penalty of death," Sean answered with a grin.

"Who else shows up to Sunday dinner?" she asked, glancing from one brother to the other. She looked as if she had been invited to something from a fairy tale.

Sam had a feeling he knew what she was asking about. "Well, since the days of our mother, you would be the first woman to get invited—other than our nanny, back in the day."

"Really?" Gina asked. Was she flattered or ready to go running off to hide in the nearest closet? "Is that a rule that your dad put in force, or just something that kind of evolved?"

"It's just the way things turned out," Sam told her, doing his best to keep the whole thing low-key.

"Then why am I being invited?" Gina asked.

"Because—" Sam shot his brother a look that had *keep quiet* written all over it "—our dad thought it might be time for a change. He said he intended to start slowly, have us take turns inviting someone over. I'm not sure if he was thinking of us or himself when it came to getting our feet wet. But since you said that you don't have any family living here, or much of one anywhere really, I'm sure if our dad met you, he'd be the first one to extend an invitation to Sunday dinner," Sam said. He paused to take a breath.

"So, how about it?" Sean jumped in. "Are you interested in coming?"

Sam felt he needed to throw her a lifeline. "Unless you're already busy or don't feel like facing six men."

"Six?" she repeated. "I thought you said there were five of you."

"Our dad is a man, too—at least, he likes to think of himself as one," Sean told her.

"Sorry. Of course he is. I meant no disrespect," she told the brothers.

"So you'll come?" Sean asked.

"By the way, whether you do or not, I'd like to hire you as my assistant," Sam told her. "This looks like a very good job," he commented, looking at the way she had organized the files thus far. He hated to admit it, but Sean was right. He did need to hire someone to help him out when it came to his practice.

"Exactly what I was thinking," Gina said. Then, as if to clarify her response, she added, "Yes to the job and yes to Sunday dinner, as well—as long as you tell me where it's at. I'm not all that great when it comes to finding my way around. I'm still somewhat new in Aurora. So, will you tell me how to get to your father's house for dinner?"

Sean grinned at the woman he considered to be his brother's new assistant. "With pleasure." Dad, Sean thought to himself, would be very happy about this turn of events. He could just feel it in his bones. He couldn't wait until his father met this gorgeous woman.

Chapter Nine

"I know my brother can be persuasive," Sam told Gina. "He's got that knack."

Some time had passed before he allowed himself to broach the subject of whatever Sean had attempted to do by talking Gina into attending Sunday dinner. Sam had already seen three patients since Sean had left the clinic.

In that time, Sam had observed Gina working, and he was rather surprised at how good she was at her new job. Her soothing manner managed to calm both the pets and their owners. One elderly woman in particular, Alice Haywood, was overly attached to her aging Lhasa Apso, whose fur was falling out in tufts. In order to comfort the woman, Gina had offered to brew some tea, then looked to Sam as if to make sure that there was some available for her to deliver.

"I have some in the kitchen cupboard," Sam recalled after a little thought.

Gina nodded. "I'll be right back," she promised the dog's "mother" and left the room.

"I don't remember seeing her before, Dr. Sterling," Alice said to Sam.

"That's because she's new," he told her.

"I thought as much," Alice said triumphantly. "Well, she seems like a lovely young lady. Mr. Gibbs took to her right away, and Mr. Gibbs is never wrong. Just how long has she been working for you?"

Sam was not in the habit of baring his soul to the owners of his patients. "Not long," he answered evasively. He kept the fact that today was Gina's first day to himself, thinking it might spoil the impression that Gina had made.

Alice nodded her head as she took in the information. "She seems like a really lovely girl, and I daresay an excellent assistant. People like that just don't come along every day, you know," the older woman told him knowingly.

Sam inclined his head. He was not about to argue the point. "No, I guess that they don't."

Gina chose that moment to return, carrying a steaming cup of tea. "I took a chance that you liked cream and sugar in your tea."

Alice smiled at Sam. "And she appears to have excellent instincts as well," she told him. Her eyes crinkled as she took the cup of hot tea from Gina. "Thank you, my dear." She looked at Sam again. "I would definitely hang on to her if I were you, Dr. Sterling. What do you say, Mr. Gibbs?" she asked her pet, fixing him with a penetrating look.

The Lhasa Apso barked emphatically at his mistress. It sounded as if he was really answering her.

Sam looked at Gina to see if she would laugh. She merely smiled warmly at the woman and her dog.

It struck Gina that there seemed to be an endless parade of pets and owners marching through the clinic that morning and afternoon. She had just a little time to visit with Charlotte between Sam's patients, and then it was back to work for her shortly thereafter.

"You really are busy," she commented to Sam after she had escorted yet another owner and their pet out of the clinic. "Why didn't you look into getting an assistant before now?" she asked, curious.

He shrugged. "I just didn't have time to interview prospective candidates until now."

"Between you and me," Gina said, "you didn't exactly have any time to conduct those interviews now, either. I just kind of happened."

Sam sighed, then laughed shortly. "You do have an infuriating way of being right."

Gina smiled. "Yes, I know. My father used to accuse me of being guilty of doing that. He was right—some of the time," she amended with a quick wink.

He had a feeling that she was telling him that he suffered in the comparison to her father. He didn't want to do anything to chase her away, so he voiced a nebulous promise. "I'll work on it."

"You don't have to do that. You being right—

when that happens—doesn't bother me," she told him honestly.

At the moment, there was a knock on the outer door, and she went over to open it. Gina found herself greeting a rather bewildered-looking man holding a leash with an iguana on the end of it. She felt as confused as he seemed to be, staring at her.

"Did I make a mistake?" the man asked, glancing around the clinic. "Has there been a change, or does Dr. Sterling still work here?"

"Dr. Sterling definitely still works here," Gina said as she looked down at his iguana. "I'm his assistant, Gina. Do you have an appointment, sir?" She would have remembered seeing the notation *iguana* on the appointment sheet.

"Don't call me *sir*," the man told her. "My name is Jake. Jake Anderson. And this," he said, smiling down at the iguana, "is Hoppy. Hoppy and I don't need an appointment. Dr. Sam said we can come in anytime we need to, and he'd make the time to see us."

Drawn by the sound of voices, Sam made his way to the front of the clinic. He smiled the moment he saw who was there.

"It's all right, Gina," he told her. "Jake was my very first walk-in when I first started up my practice. In honor of that, I told him he and Hoppy could always come in whenever Jake felt that Hoppy needed to be looked at." Sam took the older man's hand and shook it heartily. "How have you been, Jake?"

Jake cast an appreciative eye in Gina's direction. "Obviously not as good as you, Doc," he answered. And then he continued, "I think Hoppy ate something that didn't quite agree with him. Since he's an iguana, my thinking is that's not all that easy to do. But I guess it can be done."

Sam took hold of the leash, leading the iguana into the exam room. "Come with me, Hoppy. Let's see if we can't make you all better." He glanced at Gina over his shoulder. "Gina, when my next patient shows up, tell them I'll be with them as soon as I can. I'm going to finish Hoppy's examination first."

She nodded, no doubt thinking that Sam had a number of very strange patients in his practice. "Consider it done, Doctor," she said.

"Cute little thing," Jake said, looking over his shoulder at Gina as he followed Sam into the exam room. "You get her from an agency?"

"Not exactly," Sam answered.

"Then where did she come from?" the man asked, curious.

Sam was pressed for time as it was and didn't want to waste any more of it by telling Jake how he and Gina had gotten together. "It's rather a long story, Jake," Sam answered evasively.

"Some other time, then," Jake said with a nod of

his head. There was humor in his brown eyes. "When you're less busy."

Sam smiled, glad that the man wasn't attempting to argue with him. "Deal."

"Looks like she's working out well for you," Jake went on. "Does she have previous experience?"

Sam didn't answer yes or no. What he did say was "Instinct goes a long way" and left it at that as he got back to his examination of the man's longtime pet.

Things were safer that way, he had discovered.

While Sam was examining the iguana, Gina took the time to visit with her miniature collie. She fed Charlotte a little of the dog food she had discovered that was stored in the clinic for any overnight patients.

But then she heard someone ringing for the vet's attention.

Like several of the other pet owners throughout the day, this one appeared to be very bewildered by her presence. However, this one was quickly pleased to discover that the veterinarian had *finally* hired an assistant.

"I'm Marianne Johnston. My Jo-jo needs to get his shots," the woman announced, nodding at an antsy cocker spaniel. "Can I leave him with you for that while I run my errands?"

Gina had no idea what Sam's rules were when it came to leaving pets on the premises without their owners. They were going to need to go over a lot of points, she decided. This position was far more complicated than she had first thought.

"If you don't mind waiting, Ms. Johnston, let me check with Dr. Sterling. He hasn't had time to review his various rules with me. He said something about tackling them as they came up. So if you could wait right here, I'd really appreciate it," Gina told her, not giving Marianne an opening to turn her down.

As Gina slipped out of the clinic, she heard Marianne saying, "Sure, go right ahead," tacking on an "I guess" to herself.

Gina knocked on the door of the exam room that Sam had disappeared in, then walked right in. She saw the surprised look on his face, but she quickly pushed ahead. "I'm sorry to bother you, but there's a Ms. Johnston in the waiting room asking if she could leave her cocker spaniel here to get her shots while Ms. Johnston does her shopping."

To say that Sam looked nonplussed by the question was putting it mildly, but he seemed to recover well enough. "Sure, as long as she doesn't take too long. Put the cocker spaniel in the other open exam room," he instructed.

"Very good, Doctor," Gina responded and slipped out of the room.

Back in the waiting room, she told Mrs. Johnston, "Dr. Sterling said he's all right with you going to run your errands as long as you promise not to take too long. He has a very busy day ahead of him and he doesn't want Jo-jo to feel deserted or stranded."

Sam, of course, hadn't said any of this, but Gina felt she could be forgiven for winging it in this fashion. The cocker spaniel's owner would be motivated to run her errands quickly and be back at a decent time so she could pick up her pet and pay for services rendered.

"Come on, Jo-jo. Let's get you settled in while you wait for Dr. Sam," Gina told the dog, taking the leash so she could take him into the secondary exam room.

She didn't have long to wait. Gina heard the door to the other exam room closing. She quickly walked back into the lobby. "I'll take it from here, Doctor," she told Sam. "I can do the paperwork and get Hoppy here all taken care of and signed out."

Again, Sam looked surprised and then somewhat relieved a moment later. "Thank you."

"That goes for me, too," Jake told Gina, adding his thanks. Then, before Sam went to the second exam room, Jake said with a chuckle, "You should have done this years ago, Doc." He looked at Gina. "Okay, what do I owe you? What are the damages?"

Gina flipped through the paperwork that Sam had left. It was not easy to read, she thought as she squinted at it. They would need to have a talk about his penmanship as well. His notes appeared to have been made by chicken feet dipped in ink. She checked the numbers there twice before she could finally tell Jake what he owed for his iguana's visit. She expected him to put up a fuss.

Instead, he asked, "You're sure? That's all?"

Gina released the breath that she had been holding, more than a little relieved. "That's what Dr. Sterling said to charge for today's service."

Jake fairly beamed as he took out his checkbook. He kept grinning from ear to ear as he wrote out the check.

Chapter Ten

Sam had to admit that part of him hadn't expected to see Gina coming into the clinic the following morning. The salary he had offered her as his assistant was not exactly a king's ransom. In addition, the work appeared to be nonstop, and as far as he could see, Gina was working harder than he felt someone of her obvious intelligence usually did.

When he opened the clinic door for her, Sam was also surprised to see that she had brought her miniature collie with her.

The moment he unlocked the door and Gina walked in, she was talking, all but snowing him with conversation.

"I know we didn't discuss this when we talked about the job yesterday, but I don't have anywhere to leave Charlotte, and I didn't want her to be alone all day, especially right now. I noticed that there are spaces at the clinic that could easily accommodate a large dog, much less one Charlotte's size. Until I can come up with someplace to leave her while I am at work, would you mind if I brought her to the clinic with me?" Gina asked. "I would be willing to pay a boarding fee for her."

Sam bent down and ran his hands over the miniature collie's fur, saying hello to the dog. Rocky was directly behind him, dancing from foot to foot and appearing very happy to see her friend again.

"Charlotte seems like a very sweet-natured dog, and I have no problem with you bringing her to work." He petted the collie again. "Bring her with you as much as you like. It's not as if she's a vicious animal," he pointed out. "Having her here might even put some of the pet owners at ease, which would be a big plus, as far as I'm concerned."

And then he was even more straightforward with her. "To be honest, I wasn't all that certain you would be coming back today."

She looked at him, evidently somewhat confused. "Why would you think that?"

"Well, yesterday was a rather rough day, and I can't promise that every day won't be like that—or even worse," Sam told her.

"That's all right," Gina answered, waving away his concern. "I don't mind working with animals. I like it." She smiled, clearly thinking about yesterday. "Even the iguana was kind of cute."

Sam couldn't help but laugh. "You're probably the first person in history to refer to an iguana as being 'cute.'" To say that he was relieved she had decided to stay was putting the matter mildly.

"Beauty is in the eye of the beholder," Gina responded.

"I guess it must be." He glanced at his watch. It was almost time for his first appointment. "Are you ready for today's onslaught?"

Gina inclined her head. "Bring it. Just let me get Charlotte sequestered in that pet run."

"No hurry," he told her, adding, "Take your time."

But Gina returned rather quickly, glancing around the lobby. "Is Rocky in your living quarters?" she asked.

Sam nodded. "You're very observant."

"I do my best. I find that things go more smoothly when there are fewer surprises," she told him. Just then, there was a knock on the door. "And so the day begins," Gina declared.

Before she could go to open the clinic's front door, Sam asked, "How's my patient doing? Charlotte," he clarified when she looked at him blankly.

Gina smiled happily. "Charlotte has a little ways to go, but she is practically good as new."

He was glad to hear the positive report, but he did want to check it out for himself eventually. "When I get a little downtime in between patients, I'd like to reexamine Charlotte to make sure that she's healing properly."

"She is. There's no infection, and the stitches are doing just what they should," she informed him proudly. "I don't foresee any problems coming up. But of course,

I would love to have you weigh in if you get the chance. After all, you *are* the doctor."

Sam saw no reason to doubt Gina's take on the subject. This was her miniature collie, and he could see how attached she was to the animal. It would give her insight into the collie's progress. "And you appear to have the makings of an excellent assistant."

For his assessment of her abilities, Sam received a wide smile. What surprised him was his reaction to it.

He found himself completely drawn in by that smile of hers, so much so that he was totally warmed. He was secretly glad Sean had talked him into inviting Gina to attend Sunday dinner. If nothing else, it was a way to show her that he was grateful to her for all her hard work. And who knew where this would eventually lead, he mused as he watched her go to the front door.

When Gina opened it, she came eye to eye with a young woman carrying a birdcage with a cockatiel inside of it. The snow-white bird's head was all but spinning around as it took in its surroundings.

If the young woman was surprised to see that the doctor had someone working for him, she didn't show it. Her complexion was ashen as she walked in. Like her pet bird, her head was almost spinning as she looked around, searching for the veterinarian.

"Is Dr. Sam in?" the young woman asked.

"I'm right here, Dolores," Sam called as he walked

to the front of the clinic. He didn't remember her calling or leaving a message asking if she could come in, nor had he seen a notation from Gina regarding the cockatiel. "What seems to be the problem?"

The frazzled woman appeared to be almost in tears. "I think that Heather swallowed something she shouldn't have, Dr. Sterling."

"What makes you say that? Is something missing?" he asked. Picking up the bird's cage, he took a closer look at it from all angles. A tiny chain hung from the bird's small collar, but he didn't bother with it. Sam took a closer look at the cockatiel, making certain that there was a healthy space between them.

"No, I don't think that there's anything missing, at least nothing that I can see, but she's making all these strange noises, like she's swallowed something that's bothering her, and she won't eat, which isn't like her," Dolores told him.

"Well, let's have a look at you, shall we, Heather?" Sam suggested, leading the way to one of the examination rooms.

Gina noticed that the cockatiel's owner followed closely behind Sam, a hopeful expression on her face. Gina felt sorry for the young woman.

She was about to ask the veterinarian if he needed anything, but just then, she heard the bell over the clinic's front door go off again. It looked like it would be another nonstop day, Gina thought.

Sam Sterling did not need an assistant, she decided. What he really needed was a partner, someone who could pitch in and take on half the work. But it wasn't her place to suggest that. At least, not yet. But maybe, after she was further entrenched in the day-to-day dealings at the clinic, she could safely broach the subject.

She didn't foresee a warm reception to her suggestion at first, but maybe after Sam got used to the idea of having a partner, he might decide that there was some merit to it.

Gina decided to put the idea on the back burner for the time being and resurrect it when the proper time came.

If anything, today was even more fast-paced than yesterday. Gina only had a few minutes at a time to visit with Charlotte. The rest of the day, she went over billing statements, organized files and, of course, admitted patients and their owners to the clinic. She made sure that she took down the owners' statements, detailing the circumstances that had brought them and their pet to see Dr. Sterling.

Sam did send out for lunch, but finding the time to eat it was another matter entirely. Both he and Gina ate their lunches in small increments.

The hours at the clinic were from 7:00 a.m. until 7:00 p.m., although Sam told her he wasn't a stickler for ending his day exactly on time. But today, when he finished examining the last batch of patients, Sam seemed to have something on his mind other than seeing another patient.

"Would you be able to stay after hours?" he asked her as the last pet and their owner walked out of the clinic.

"Do you have something you need organized?" Gina asked, saying the first thing that came to her mind.

"Not exactly," Sam answered evasively.

When he stated it that way, she wasn't sure what to think. "Then what, 'exactly'?" Gina asked.

"How are you when it comes to doing inventory?" Sam asked.

Of course there were things he needed to have on hand to do his work properly. "You tell me what you want me to note down, and I'll be on the lookout for it," she volunteered.

Sam looked at her, bemused. "Don't you have any plans for tonight?" he asked, curious.

Gina shrugged. Since moving out here a little more than six months ago, she still had not built up much of a network of friends. Quite honestly, she felt that it was just her and her miniature collie. She was beyond grateful to Sam for saving Charlotte. Actually, she had been thinking about going to work for a veterinarian or at an animal clinic, so this whole situation could not have turned out better for her if she had planned it. So it went without saying that she was more than happy to help Sam out with anything he might need in order to run his clinic.

"Nothing that can't be bent or worked around," she told him freely.

"I guess that makes me a very lucky employer," he told her.

"I guess that it does," Gina agreed. "At any rate, working for you has me more than willing to move things around. As far as I'm concerned, this job comes first—before anything else."

She had clearly impressed him. "Not many of you people left."

"I wouldn't know. I haven't exactly taken inventory. I just know how I feel about working with animals and about working with you as a veterinarian since you devote your time to working with animals. So, whatever you need, Dr. Sterling," she told him, "consider it done." The bell rang at the front door. "However, at the moment, I think that you have another patient who needs your attention," she informed him.

"I do believe you're right. Let me get that one," Sam said, then added with a smile, "For old times' sake."

She raised her hands as if in cheerful surrender. "By all means. I won't stand in your way. Seeing you might just reassure your patient's owner." She followed up with a broad wink.

Sam laughed under his breath, then went to answer the door while Gina busied herself with the work she had left out on her desk.

But while she worked, she waited for the veterinarian to call her over. She was ready to drop everything if and when he needed her when it came to working with the animals.

Chapter Eleven

By the time Friday rolled around, Gina found that she had gotten into a comfortable routine when it came to her work as a veterinarian's assistant.

She knew her way around the clinic and knew how much time Sam needed when it came to treating dogs, cats or birds, be they parrots, canaries or cockatiels. And there was the occasional hamster and, of course, the iguana. Without disturbing the clinic's supplies, she managed to arrange them so she could get her hands on them quickly should Sam have need of them. After a while, Gina felt that she had arranged everything.

Something else she had noticed over the last few days, with Rocky roaming around the area before the clinic was open and after it was closed, was that the German shepherd lost a great deal of fur. Evidence of that loss was everywhere to be seen, yet Rocky did not appear to be missing fur anywhere in particular on her body.

So on Friday, Gina, having been given her own key to the clinic, arrived early. She'd brought a cordless vacuum cleaner with her and moved around the clinic, cleaning up the tufts of fur that had gotten embedded in the floorboards. She definitely had no patience when it came to messy spaces, Gina thought, working as quickly as she could.

She was so preoccupied with getting the German shepherd's fur cleaned up, she didn't even hear Sam coming into the clinic. So when he came up behind her and asked "What are you doing?" it took a lot for her not to jump and emit a high-pitched scream of surprise. What she did do was swing around and come very close to hitting the veterinarian with her vacuum cleaner.

"You shouldn't sneak up on someone like that," Gina told him sharply, doing her best to breathe normally so that he wouldn't realize just how much he had thrown her off. She pressed her hand against her chest to keep her pounding heart from leaping out.

"I didn't realize I was sneaking," Sam told her. "But you still haven't answered me. What are you doing?"

Gina looked at him incredulously. "I would have thought that would be self-evident," she answered. "I'm vacuuming up the fur that seems to have fallen off your dog as she runs around the clinic, as well as the ground level of your private quarters. The fur is so light that it's hard to notice when it's falling at first. But if you sweep it up, you can see that Rocky seems to lose a ton of it—all the time," she told him with a wave of her hand. "To be honest, I'm surprised that you don't have a bald dog by now. From all indications, Rocky has lost enough fur to build you another dog this week alone."

"Well, she has lost a great deal of fur," Sam agreed. "But it's not up to you to clean up after my pet. I certainly don't expect you to do that."

"I understand that, but the truth of it is, I really don't like working in a messy area. I've never been able to think clearly under those conditions." Gina smiled at him. "Just accept it as a bonus for hiring me on as your assistant."

"Well, if I can't talk you out of it—because I really doubt that I can—I'm going to have to compensate you for the time and effort you spend cleaning up Rocky's fur," Sam told her.

Gina's smile widened. "Well, we can certainly discuss that," she told him amicably. She glanced at her watch. "But that's all I can do for now. Your first patient should be arriving soon."

Just then, the doorbell to the clinic rang.

Gina grinned as she retired the vacuum cleaner, setting it behind a closet door. "Here's your first patient, right on cue," she declared.

"Let me get that," Sam offered, turning to walk through the clinic to the front door.

"Hell no. You're the doctor, I'm the assistant. It's up to me to assist," she said, striding past him.

She opened the clinic's door to a well-dressed

woman holding a cat in a pet carrier with one hand and what looked to be her four-year-old daughter's hand with the other. Gina immediately went to take the pet carrier from the woman. The cat didn't appear to be very happy about the transfer and made a loud hissing sound.

"You must be Mrs. Mullins, and this must be Fluffy," Gina said, looking at the cat in the pet carrier. And then she turned to look at the little girl, who appeared to be attempting to hide behind her mother. "And who is this very pretty little helper with you?" Gina asked, smiling down at the little girl.

The little girl's expression changed. She raised her head proudly, her curly blond hair swinging back and forth around her face. "My name is Shelly," she announced.

"Well, it's very nice to meet you, Shelly," Gina told the child. "Why don't you and your mommy come with me, and we'll all take Fluffy here into the exam room so that Dr. Sam can take a look at her and see what he needs to do to make her all better? Would you like that?"

Shelly's head bobbed up and down enthusiastically, and she said solemnly, "That would be very nice, won't it, Mommy? To have Fluffy all better."

"It would be very nice," her mother answered with genuine feeling. She looked slightly tired. Taking care of Fluffy and her daughter was obviously taking a lot out of the woman.

Gina brought mother, daughter and cat to the first exam room. "Let me put the pet carrier on the examination table, and then I'll go tell Dr. Sam that you're all here," she told Mrs. Mullins. She was about to leave the room when the little girl caught her hand. Rather than pull her hand away, Gina looked down at her quizzically.

"Are you new here?" Shelly asked.

"Not as new as I was," Gina answered with a smile.

The answer did not satisfy the little girl. "Does that mean that you're going to go on working here?"

"Well, that's all up to Dr. Sam, but I would certainly like to," Gina answered.

Shelly nodded her head solemnly, then smiled as if deciding she had taken a shine to her. "I'll tell Dr. Sam to keep you," she told Gina.

Gina took that as serious input. "Thank you, Shelly. I'm sure Dr. Sam would definitely appreciate your opinion on the subject," she told her. Out of the corner of her eye, Gina saw that Mrs. Mullins was smiling broadly at her.

She opened the door to tell Sam that his patient's family was waiting to talk to him—and almost walked directly into him.

Gina flushed. "Sorry," she apologized. "I guess that was just a little too much enthusiasm."

Sam had caught hold of her shoulders to keep them from colliding. Despite that, he told her, "There's nothing wrong with enthusiasm. Enthusiasm keeps the job fresh and you interested in it."

Gina cleared her throat, embarrassed at the near collision. "That's always been my feeling," she told him. As the doorbell sounded again, she said to Sam, "That's my signal. I'll leave you to Fluffy and her family."

Just as Gina slipped out of the room, Shelly stuck her head out, apparently looking for her. Gina paused. "Can I help you?" she asked the little girl.

Shelly's head bobbed up and down. "Dr. Sam said you had a pet dog. Can I see him?"

"It's a her," Gina corrected. "And of course you can." Charlotte was very good with people. Especially children. Gina decided that the patient in the clinic could wait a few minutes. "As long as it's all right with your mother," she said.

"She said it was okay," Shelly told her proudly. The little girl shyly tucked her hand into Gina's.

A warm feeling slipped over Gina. Someday, she thought, she wanted to have a little girl—or boy—of her own. One who was as animated as this little person was, Gina thought fondly. But that day was undoubtedly still very far away.

"Charlotte's right in here," she told Shelly, leading her into the room.

Shelly appeared both fascinated and a little hesitant, but the latter lasted only long enough for Gina to bring her fully into the room.

"Can I pet her?" Shelly asked, wide-eyed and eager.

Gina took hold of Charlotte's collar, making sure that she wouldn't rear up unexpectedly. "Charlotte," she said by way of an introduction, "this is Shelly. I expect you to be on your very best behavior," she told the miniature collie. Bringing the dog closer to the little girl while holding tightly to her collar, she said, "Say hi to Shelly, Charlotte."

Shelly reached up, clearly wanting to pet the collie. "Is it all right?" she asked.

"Charlotte is a little overeager, but she really likes to be petted," Gina told the little girl.

Shelly ran her hand along the dog's fur, slowly at first, then with enthusiasm. The smile on her face was almost blinding. "She's as soft as my kitty," she declared happily as she continued petting Charlotte.

"Yes, she is. Okay, Charlotte," Gina told her pet. "Shelly needs to go back to her mommy now, and I have to get back to work." She looked at the little girl. "Say goodbye to Charlotte, Shelly."

"Goodbye, Charlotte," Shelly declared obediently, petting the miniature collie one last time. Then she slid her hand into Gina's again, indicating that she was ready to return to her mother and her cat waiting for her in the examination room.

"Shelly wanted to come back to see how her pet is doing," Gina told Mrs. Mullins and Sam as she opened the door so Shelly could walk into the room.

Just then, Gina heard the doorbell ring again. "They're

playing my song," she told Shelly with a smile. "I'm going to have to talk to whoever is waiting to see Dr. Sam." Then she slipped out of the room, closing the door behind her.

There was nothing remarkable about the next patient and owner who arrived, or the patient and owner who arrived after that.

The ensuing parade of patients kept Gina on her toes for the next few hours, although she did find the time to pause and wave goodbye to Shelly as the little girl left with her mother and cat. But that was only because Gina had to write up the bill for the visit and collect the money for the cat's exam plus the medication that Sam had prescribed.

Just as in the previous days, although Sam ordered lunch for them both, they had to work through that time period until there was a break in the rush of animals who came into the clinic. They finally had an opportunity to eat almost three hours later.

"I have to tell you," Sam said as they sat down to eat, "all the clients who came in today were even more impressed with you than the ones from previous days. Mrs. Mullins wanted to know why I hadn't hired you sooner."

"Did you tell her that you didn't know me sooner?" Gina asked with a laugh.

"I don't think she's the kind who accepts any excuses," Sam told her.

Just then, the doorbell rang. Sam and Gina sighed loudly in unison.

"I guess it's back to work," Gina declared, getting to her feet and heading toward the front door.

Chapter Twelve

When she learned that Sam put in hours at the clinic on Saturdays, Gina had to admit that she was not surprised. A little overwhelmed, perhaps, but when she thought about it, she had to admit that it seemed par for the course.

"You didn't sign on for six days a week," he pointed out when she surprised him by coming into the clinic on Saturday. She had driven by on a hunch that he might be working, just to discover that she was right.

"Not outright, no," she agreed. "But since you're working Saturdays, then I am, too. At the very least, I should be working with you at the clinic on Saturdays in the beginning. If I wear out," she threw in, cocking her head to look at him a bit more closely, "we'll renegotiate. How's that?"

Sam couldn't help laughing at the idea that this woman was actually opting for more work. Part of him was convinced that he had to be dreaming this. He looked at her and shrugged. "I'm not about to turn you down, if that's what you're waiting for, although

I have a difficult time believing that you really *want* to work six days a week."

"Why?" she asked incredulously. "*You* work six days a week."

"This is my business, and working these hours is what I choose to do to make a go of that business," Sam pointed out.

Gina smiled up at him, utterly composed. "Well, since you put it that way, so do I."

Sam took a breath. For now, he would leave things the way they were. He could revisit this topic later, and he was sure that by then, she would have changed her mind about working Saturdays. Right now, there was something else he needed to talk to her about.

"At the risk of alienating you," he began, watching her face carefully, "are you still willing to have Sunday dinner at my father's house tomorrow?"

She wasn't sure how to take his question. Had he changed his mind about bringing her? Only one way to find out, she thought. She had to ask him outright. "Are you trying to get out of it?" Gina asked.

"No, I am *not*. As a matter of fact, nothing is further from the truth," Sam told her. "I called my father last night to broach the idea that I was bringing someone—"

She immediately jumped to what she assumed was his father's reaction. "And was he upset?" she asked. This was, after all, a family tradition, and she was definitely not family. It wouldn't be a stretch to guess that the family patriarch wouldn't want a stranger at his table. Her attendance had been Sam's brother's idea.

"Upset?" Sam asked incredulously. His eyes narrowed as he stared at her. Was she joking? "My father was overjoyed to hear the news. I can tell you that he said something about being thrilled to have a new person with fresh dialogue sitting at his table."

Gina regarded him dubiously. He had to be pulling her leg. "Oh, I sincerely doubt your father was overjoyed to hear that your new assistant was coming to Sunday dinner."

"Well, you can judge that for yourself when you come tomorrow," he told her. "I've got your address," he said, thinking of the tax forms she'd filled out when he took her on as his assistant. "I'll be by to pick you up at 2:30, if that's okay with you. Dinner starts at three o'clock—give or take a few minutes."

But Gina shook her head. "You don't have to do that, Dr. Sterling," she told him formally. "Just give me your father's address and I can drive to his house myself."

It was Sam's turn to shake his head. "Oh, no, I was instructed by my father to bring you, at least to your first Sunday dinner, so that's what I intend to do. Bring you," he emphasized. He lowered his head to confide, "Between you and me, I think my father is worried that you'll change your mind about coming and decide not to show up at the last minute. So, at least this first time, I will escort you to my father's house. The house, in case you're interested, where all five of us grew up."

She nodded, hiding the smile that rose to her lips. "Yes, I believe you did mention that."

"I did, didn't I?" he realized. For a moment, he looked embarrassed. "Sorry, this is all rather new to me."

She wasn't sure just what he was referring to. "What, talking to a woman? I've seen you talking to women, Dr. Sterling."

He was referring to bringing someone over to Sunday dinner, but first he wanted to clear up her confusion. "What you've seen, Gina, is me talking to my patients' owners," he pointed out. "And there are no patients here at the moment. So in the interest of not being awkward, you can call me Sam. I think we would both feel more comfortable if you did that."

"You're the boss," she told him. And then she rolled it over in her mind. "You're right. Calling you Sam does roll more easily off my tongue than Dr. Sterling, but ultimately, it's your call."

And then she heard the doorbell ring. The first one of the day, she thought. Gina pulled her shoulders back as she turned toward the front door. "Sounds like they're playing our song, Dr. Sterling," she told him with a wink.

He caught himself reacting to her wink. It took him a second to pull back mentally and focus again.

"I guess you'd better go and answer that. I'll be in Exam Room One." He turned on his heel.

He was only partially aware of the smile on his lips. Who would have known six days ago when he woke up to that pounding on his door that his life would wind up changing so much? Certainly not him, Sam thought. And right now, it felt as if his life was constantly transforming. For the last six days, ever since he'd opened his door to that distraught-looking young woman, he hadn't known what to expect, or more to the point, exactly just what to brace himself for.

Walking past a window as he prepared to see his first patient of the day, Sam caught a glimpse of his reflection. Damn, but he was actually grinning. He couldn't remember the last time he had grinned, or even the last time he had actually wanted to.

He blew out a breath as he waited for the exam room door to open. Gina had certainly turned things around and set everything on its ear. Sunday, he decided, was shaping up to be one hell of a day.

The exam room door opened, and Sam cleared his mind to focus on his first patient of the day.

She couldn't get her heart to stop pounding, Gina realized. Thinking back, she honestly couldn't remember the last time she had gone out on a date. Not that this was actually considered a date, she reminded herself.

All right, if it's not a date, what would you call it? Gina asked herself the following morning.

Well, you could call it Sunday afternoon, she told herself.

"You're making too much out of it," she said out loud. "This is just a simple dinner at your boss's house. It's just his way of saying thank you. No big deal."

Just because her last employer was a clod bent on working the people at his company to death, it didn't mean Sam was like that, because he certainly wasn't. Unlike her old boss, Sam's first thought was not about how much money he could collect; it was about how much he could help his patients. Money came last, and despite the economy, his fees didn't reflect high prices. The first thing that had struck her, other than the fact that the man had a great smile and was very good-looking in a dark, brooding way, was that he was hardworking and conscientious.

The unexpected thought that Sam was good-looking caught Gina by surprise. How had that managed to sneak in?

She supposed she was so grateful to Sam for taking care of Charlotte and sewing up all of her wounds that she had just kind of naturally become attracted to the man.

You're making too much out of this, she told herself, annoyed that she couldn't control her thoughts. *This is what happens when you haven't dated since Noah collected two of everything to herd onto his ark.*

Blowing out a breath, Gina looked herself over in the mirror that hung in her small bedroom. Maybe she should have put on the red dress, she thought. It was a little more flattering. The blue dress looked too subdued. But the red was too loud.

Gina looked over at her cell phone. Maybe she should call Sam and tell him something had come up and she wouldn't be able to make it to dinner.

"You're going to have to back up your story. You told Sam that you didn't know anyone who lived here and your sister lived somewhere else. You don't have a viable excuse—unless you just suddenly up and quit," she mocked herself. "C'mon. Since when did you become such a coward?"

She had painted herself right into a corner.

"You don't run from things, remember? So what is your problem?" she challenged. And then it suddenly hit her. The reason she was being so skittish was that she was actually attracted to the man.

"Okay," she told herself. "Picture Sam as being ugly."

Gina frowned. That wasn't the answer. She wasn't the type to be attracted to just looks. She decided to change her approach.

"Picture him like being straight out of a horror movie. A being with an ugly soul," she told her reflection in the hanging mirror.

Gina blew out a breath and shook her head. "It's official. For whatever reason, you have just gone off the deep end. Maybe you should hand in your resignation so that you don't take Sam down with you."

The woman in the mirror looked back at her skeptically. Gina sighed. "Yeah, yeah, I'm just babbling," she said to her reflection. "This is what happens when you don't get out often enough—or at all."

But that still didn't manage to calm her nerves. She needed a different solution.

Gina glanced at her car keys. Maybe there was still enough time for her to get away before Sam arrived. Yes, it was cowardly, but she'd sort all that out later. She grabbed her keys, her purse and slipped on her shoes. She made it all the way to the front door—and that was when the doorbell rang.

There was no back door, Gina thought as a feeling of being trapped washed over her, engulfing her. She supposed she could stay very still and pretend that she wasn't in, but if the man had eyes, he would see her car parked right out front.

Bracing herself, Gina blew out another breath. How bad could it be? She looked back at Charlotte. "Say a prayer for Mommy," she instructed.

The moment she opened the door, Sam's neutral expression melted away into an appreciative smile. "Wow," he told her. "You really look great."

The compliment threw her. "Thank you," she murmured, picking up her purse.

Sam glanced around the room. What was he looking for?

"Where's Charlotte?" he asked her.

She thought that was a strange thing to ask. "I guess in the bedroom. Why?"

Sam smiled at her. "Because she's coming with us."

Gina looked at him, stunned. This man was really full of surprises. "She is?"

"Of course she is. You don't want to leave her alone, do you?" he asked. Almost as if he wanted Gina to feel as comfortable as possible and he knew having her pet with her would accomplish just that.

And right then and there, with those very simple words, Sam Sterling completely won over his heretofore very nervous veterinarian assistant.

"I'll go get Charlotte's leash and be right back," she told him happily.

"I'll be right here," Sam called after her.

Chapter Thirteen

"Are you sure about this?" Gina asked. Sam was driving both her and her miniature collie to his father's house, and she was still struggling with doubts about the wisdom of doing this. What if his father decided for some reason he didn't like her? Would that put her job in jeopardy?

"Sure about what?" Sam asked, sparing Gina a quick glance. "You're going to have to be a little more specific."

She took a deep breath. "Don't you think that springing someone new on your father for what is normally a traditional Sunday dinner is already a bit much for him? Throwing a strange dog into the mix might push this visit right over the top, wouldn't it?" She glanced at her dog in the back seat. "I mean, Charlotte is normally a very gentle dog, but I can't guarantee how she might react to a room full of men she's never met before. She might feel hemmed in."

Sam laughed. It had only been a week, but she knew he had already built up a good relationship with the miniature collie. "I'm sure Charlotte will react just fine. I got my love of animals—especially dogs—from my father. And my mother," he added deliberately. "You don't need to worry. It'll be fine." He smiled at her reassuringly. "I give you my word."

Gina turned around in her seat. She was fairly certain that Sam had installed the special seat belt in the back for his own German shepherd. Right now, Charlotte was putting the seat belt to use and seemed quite comfortable. "I feel bad that you have to leave Rocky at home."

"Trust me, she gets spoiled enough. And just so you know, I don't always bring Rocky to Sunday dinner. My dad requires that his sons turn up, but having their pets there is optional."

"Pets," Gina repeated. "Do all your brothers have dogs?" It hadn't even occurred to her to ask before.

"Just two of them, Sebastian and Scott," Sam told her. "And in case you're wondering, I passed the word along to my brothers that my guest would be bringing her miniature collie with her, so in the interest of tranquility, I suggested that they leave their dogs home."

"That must have gone over like a lead balloon," Gina commented dryly.

"Like I said, the dogs don't always come. And actually, they were a lot more interested in the fact that I was bringing someone to Sunday dinner," he told her. "I explained that you were my new assistant and that you were relatively new in Aurora, so I was bringing you to dinner as a way of saying thank you for all your help."

"Then this really is a first, you bringing someone to dinner?" Gina asked. Part of her had thought that he was exaggerating that fact just to get her to agree. Another part of her felt a little disappointed that this didn't mean anything more than a thank-you. "Nobody else ever showed up at your table? Nobody new?" she asked incredulously. She was starting to feel even more nervous about the whole thing.

"Thinking back, I have to say no, nobody new ever turned up for Sunday dinner." And then he paused as if remembering something. "Nobody new other than Randi, our nanny slash housekeeper, I mean. Randi used to attend Sunday dinners with us for years. She's part of the family, and she also really isn't. After we all graduated from college, Randi moved into her own place not far away. She still turns up at Sunday dinners on occasion, and I have to admit, things always tend to go a lot more smoothly when she does." Sam smiled fondly. "Randi always knows how to move the conversation along when it suddenly stops."

"Will she be there?" Gina asked hopefully.

"Not this Sunday," Sam responded matter-of-factly. "If you decided you want to do this again, I'm sure she'll put in an appearance somewhere along the line."

"If?" she questioned. That didn't sound very promising, she thought. Was he expecting her to be turned off after tonight?

"Well, no one is going to hold a gun to your head," he told her. "Just wanted you to know that coming back was an option—and to show you how grateful I am that this little venture turned out to be positive." He pulled up in front of a two-story house that was far from new but kept up impressively well. "I didn't know what I was missing until you turned up."

Was he flattering her, or was she making too much out of his comment? She honestly didn't know, but she didn't want to allow herself to get carried away. Finding out that she'd misunderstood would be awkwardly painful.

Belatedly, she realized they had stopped moving. She took in the house for the first time. "Are we here?" she asked Sam.

"Yes," he answered with an amused grin, "we're here." It hit him that he was smiling a lot more. That had to be because of Gina, he thought. And, he concluded, it felt good.

Getting out of the car, he circled around to the passenger side. He opened Gina's door for her, but rather than give her his arm to guide her out, he stepped to the rear and unbuckled the dog's seat belt. He took great care to make sure he was holding on to Charlotte's leash so she didn't bolt unexpectedly. This was a new location for the dog, and he didn't want her getting frightened and running off. After all, she didn't know the area—yet.

Gina was impressed with the care Sam was showing her dog. Yes, he was a veterinarian, but that didn't mean he had to treat her miniature collie as if she was special.

"I can take her leash," Gina told him.

"That's all right. I'll hang on to her for now. You did point out that this will all be new to her, so I don't want Charlotte getting skittish. It shouldn't take her long to get used to the surrounding area as well as to my family."

Gina held up both of her hands. "You know best."

"Much as I would like to bask in that heady sentiment, I really don't. I just happen to know this situation," Sam told her. Keeping a hold on Charlotte's leash, he led the way to the front door, where he surprised Gina by handing her a key ring. "Why don't you open the door? I want to be able to keep my hands free," he explained.

Gina looked at him, taken aback. "Don't you think I should just ring the doorbell, seeing as how I've never been here before? If your dad sees me first, he might think I'm a burglar."

"With a key?" Sam questioned, clearly amused. He was focused on trying to keep Charlotte calm. This was, after all, someplace new for the miniature collie, and she was reacting to the confusing potpourri of different smells.

Gina shrugged at the skepticism in his voice. "There are burglars who manage to get keys to a house," she protested.

"Do me a favor—if and when you happen to meet Randi, don't mention that," Sam responded. "The woman has a vivid imagination, and she has a tendency to worry too much."

Gina nodded. "Understood. And you, young lady," she said, bending down and addressing her antsy pet, "make sure you stay on your best behavior. Okay?"

Charlotte cocked her head, acting as if she was absorbing every word her mistress was saying to her.

With that, and against her better judgment, Gina inserted the key into the lock and pushed open the door. Sam was still holding on to Charlotte's leash, but with the door open, the miniature collie's excitement intensified. Sam still managed to keep her in check, although Gina knew it wasn't as easy as one would think, given the dog's size.

"We're here, Dad," Sam called out.

One minute later, an older, slightly more distinguished version of Sam walked into the modest entrance hall. His full head of hair was iron gray rather than Sam's midnight black. The man's face, given his age and vocation, was amazingly unlined.

"So I see." Bright blue eyes crinkled as Sanford Sterling bent down and petted the eager dog.

Charlotte was fighting to get on her hind legs in order to lick Sam's father's face.

"Hello, girl. Aren't you pretty?" Sanford noted appreciatively. He petted the dog's head with gentle enthusiasm, then raised his eyes to look at the young woman standing beside his son. "And you must be Gina," he said warmly by way of greeting.

"I must be," Gina affirmed, smiling back at him. She had been prepared to be intimidated. Instead, she found herself charmed. She put out her hand at the same time that Sam's father did. "It's very nice to meet you, Mr. Sterling."

Sanford smiled, and Gina felt that she had a glimpse of what Sam would look like in the future. "It's terrific to meet you, Miss..."

"Please, call me Gina," she requested. Having her boss's father refer to her in such a formal way just didn't seem right.

Sanford inclined his head. "Gina," he repeated. It was obvious that he welcomed abandoning formality. "Tell me, how did you talk my stubborn son into hiring you as his assistant?" Before she could frame an answer, he went on with feeling, "You have no idea how long I have been after him to do that. Practically from the day he began his veterinary practice."

Sam clapped a genial hand on his father's shoulder. "Why don't we save that for the table, Dad, so Gina doesn't have to repeat herself half a dozen times to fill in Simon, Scott, Sean and Sebastian?"

It suddenly occurred to Gina that, except for the brother who'd turned up at his clinic that first emotion-filled day, she still wasn't sure she knew all of them. "Are those your brothers' names?" she asked.

His father looked at Sam, feigning disappointment.

"You didn't tell her your brothers' names? Talk about throwing someone in the middle of the pool without their water wings. Come," Sanford urged Gina, escorting his new guest into the oversize living room.

Seated on the sofa, in the midst of conversation, were four young men who eerily resembled one another. Gina recognized one of them: Sean, the one she had met that first day when she decided to help Sam with his files. As she recalled, he was the youngest of the Sterling brothers. It was Sean who had invited her to attend their Sunday dinner. Who knew? If not for him, she might have not come after all and perhaps not even been motivated to work for Sam. One thing had certainly led to another. She owed Sam's youngest brother a lot, she thought.

Sean rose to his feet ahead of his other brothers. "So, you decided to come after all," he said, sounding pleased. "Glad to see that my big brother had the good sense to hire you and bring you here to the old homestead. Sam has a tendency to resist suggestions that make sense most of the time," Sean told her. "Maybe while you put his files in order, you can teach him how to be less uptight."

"I think Charlotte is working on that last part," she answered.

"Charlotte?" another brother asked, confused. "Who's Charlotte?"

"This lovely lady right here," their father said, bringing the miniature collie into the living room.

"Ah, it figures," the brother said, nodding his head at the animal.

"Well, boys—and girl," the senior Sterling said, his eyes sweeping over the people gathered in his living room. "What do you say we all file into the dining room, where we can carry on this conversation over a healthy serving of mashed potatoes, mixed vegetables and baked spareribs?"

"That sounds wonderful," Gina told him.

Sanford's sons said nothing. They were too busy making their way into the dining room. All except for Sam, who remained beside her. "Careful they don't trample you," he warned. "Hot meals have a way of doing that to them."

Gina nodded. "Duly noted."

Chapter Fourteen

Gina had assumed that conversation at the dinner table would be slow moving and at times possibly even nonexistent. After all, she was a stranger to most of the men in Sam's family, and in her experience, men weren't always quick to warm up to strangers.

Much to her relief, less than ten minutes into her visit she discovered that this was not the case. She found to her delight that she was greatly entertained by the conversation taking place all around her. Moreover, the Sterling men were going out of their way to pull her into it. She was charmed that they all seemed to be in competition for her attention. She gave it to all of them.

This was not the experience that Sam had painted for her to expect. There was no downtime, no awkward breaks in the chatter. If anything, Sam turned out to be the quiet one. His father and younger brothers were definitely more talkative.

And the food, Gina discovered, was incredibly delicious.

"This is wonderful," she told Sam's father after she

had sampled everything. The menu had completely whetted her appetite, and each forkful just kept getting better. "Did you have this catered from a restaurant?"

Sanford exchanged looks with Sean, sitting to his right. "Did I have this catered from a restaurant?" he repeated and then laughed. "I'm sorry. I didn't mean to laugh at your question," he quickly apologized. "But in all honesty it did strike me as funny. Let me explain. In honor of my late wife, I taught all my sons how to cook and bake," he told her. "Getting our sons to be self-sufficient was extremely important to her. And preparing meals also taught them the value of a dollar. As you know, making your own meals costs a great deal less than having ready-made meals brought to you. So the boys take turns making Sunday dinner," the man informed Gina proudly.

"Which one of you made this dinner?" she asked, scanning the faces of the five young men at the table.

Simon, the divorce lawyer, raised his hand. "That would be me."

"These have to be the best spareribs I've ever had," Gina told him with enthusiasm. "You should be very proud of yourself."

Simon shrugged off her compliment as if embarrassed by it. "Pride has nothing to do with it. It's a matter of practicality."

"Practicality?" Gina questioned, slightly confused. She could think of a lot of words that might be applicable to this family meal, but *practicality* was not one of them.

"What Simon is saying," Sean said patiently, "is that he doesn't want to starve to death, so for him cooking is a simple matter of practical survival. It seems that being a divorce lawyer has completely soured him on the notion that love is a lasting emotion. So knowing how to get around in the kitchen is extremely necessary."

"He's not serious, is he?" Gina questioned, turning toward Sam. The lawyer's philosophy sounded like a terrible way to approach life.

"Oh, Simon is most definitely serious," Sean told her, following his remark with a broad wink that only served to confuse Gina even further.

"Better to be safe than sorry and stripped of all my worldly possessions," Simon told her. "You have no idea what I've managed to witness in my profession. I have seen dewy-eyed women who swore undying love go on to all but eviscerate the same men they pledged their troth to. Those women try their best to separate the men from their money."

"Other than that, Simon is a happy-go-lucky kind of guy," Sam told her, then laughed.

Gina looked at Sam, not sure if he was putting her on. "I'll take your word for it," she said, thinking that was a safe enough response.

"Hey, don't let Simon dampen your spirits," said Sebastian. He was the next-to-youngest brother and, in everyone's opinion, the brilliant one in the family. Sebastian had completed bachelor's and master's degrees in Shakespearean literature before the age of twenty and had then gone on to become a professor at that same local university while putting up with his brothers' endless teasing. "We've learned to put up with his sour take on things."

"Speak for yourself, pretty boy," Simon said to Sebastian. "I'm not sour—I just happen to see things clearly."

"Yeah, right. Clear as mud," Scott scoffed. "If everyone shared your cheerful take on things, civilization as we know it would die off in less than a generation." He made a dour face at his brother.

"Don't mind them," Sam said, bending his head and whispering in Gina's ear. "Like I said, we don't have guests over for Sunday dinner. It took me a few minutes to figure out what these numbskulls are doing, but they're all clearly showing off for you."

"Oh, I really doubt that," Gina said, waving away his take on the situation. "But if that's actually the case, I have to tell you I'm flattered." She flashed a wide, warm smile as she looked around at all the handsome faces surrounding her. To a man, beginning with Sanford, the Sterling men were all extremely good-looking.

"Hey, big brother, tell us. Where did you find this lovely lady?" Scott asked, nodding at Gina.

"Yeah, and why haven't we ever met her before? Where have you been hiding her?" Sebastian asked.

"Hey, if you were Sam, would you want to bring her here to this crowded man-fest?" Sean asked, looking around the table.

"To answer your question, I 'found' Gina when she came pounding on my door in the middle of the night on Sunday or early Monday morning, take your pick," Sam informed his brothers.

Scott rolled his eyes. "Now he has gorgeous women pounding on his door. Boy, some guys have all the luck."

"It's not what you think," Gina said, noticing the smiles on their faces as they looked from her to Sam. "My miniature collie was attacked by a pit bull while I was walking her. That vicious animal did a terrible number on her. Someone had given me your brother's name and number and said he was an extremely good veterinarian who could practically work miracles."

"Well, I can't deny that Sam is that," Simon agreed, begrudgingly nodding his head.

"Hey, I've got a question," Sean said, raising his hand.

Gina turned in his direction. "And that is?"

"How did you get that pit bull to let go of your dog?" he asked. "From everything Sam has ever told us, pit bulls don't just calmly walk away. Once they sink their teeth into another animal, they won't just let go."

Gina smiled. "They do if you pelt them with a lot of rocks. I was lucky there was a park nearby with a rock garden. I just kept throwing rocks at that dog until he finally ran away. And then I wrapped Charlotte up in a blanket, carried her to my car and brought her straight to the clinic. I was just lucky that your brother lived behind the clinic." She glanced gratefully at Sam. "I don't know what I would have done if he didn't."

"There's a twenty-four-hour animal hospital located a couple of miles from the middle of the city," Sanford volunteered. "You could have taken your collie there."

"I'm relatively new in this city. I didn't know about the hospital," Gina answered. "And at the time, I was really desperate. Charlotte was bleeding a great deal, and I couldn't get her to stop. I have to admit that I was really scared."

"Well, you couldn't have found a better veterinarian to take care of your pet than Sam," Sanford told her with pride.

"Yeah. Much as I hate to admit it, Dad's right." Sean added his voice to his father's.

"A compliment? From you?" Sam asked, pretending to be amazed. "Either I'm dying or you are."

Sean gave him a look that was clearly supposed to put Sam in his place. "And this is why I don't give you compliments, big brother."

"Boys, you're supposed to be on your best behavior around our guest," Sanford chided, suppressing a smile.

"Uh-oh, Dad means business. He's using his stern voice to get us to act politely." Sean winked at Gina. "I guess this means we'd better behave."

Sanford looked at Gina. "This is why we don't have guests over at our house. I always worry that a few minutes of this and anyone would go running out of the house, hands over their ears and screaming." He chuckled. "I must say, you've lasted a great deal longer than I thought you would when Sam told me he was going to be bringing you to dinner."

Gina smiled. She didn't need to pretend. She was really having a good time and didn't mind showing it. "You know, this is just as I would have imagined Sunday dinner being like with a family. It makes me regret that I didn't have a bunch of brothers or sisters myself," she said honestly.

"Are you an only child?" Sebastian asked her curiously.

Gina didn't bother hiding her sadness. "I have a sister," she admitted, "but for all that's worth, I might as well be an only child."

"Huh. I wish I was an only child," Simon declared wistfully.

Before his brothers could agree with him, Gina quickly said, "No, you don't. You guys have a good thing going. There's nothing like family to make you feel loved and a part of something." She glanced around the table, pinning them down with a look. "Both in good times and in bad."

"If you don't mind my asking, how would you know?" Simon asked innocently. "I mean, seeing that for all intents and purposes, you feel like an only child."

Gina smiled at him. "I guess I just have a great imagination."

Sean looked toward his father. "Can we keep her, Dad?" he asked in a singsong voice. "I promise to feed her and walk her and take really good care of her. Please, Dad?"

Sanford laughed, shaking his head, as if pleased with the cheerful atmosphere. "I think you need to take that up with Sam—and with Gina, of course."

"Sam is a spoilsport," Sean complained with a dramatic sigh. "How about it, Gina? Are you willing to stay with us? You won't regret it. You won't even have to work."

"I like to work," Gina pointed out.

"You're being creepy, little brother," Sam told Sean.

"But truthful," Sean countered with a large grin.

Simon laughed dismissively. "Don't pay any attention to Sean, Gina. He fancies himself a Romeo."

"He's nothing like Romeo," Sebastian said, speaking up. "If any of you had ever read *Romeo and Juliet*, you would know that."

Sam turned toward Gina. "Had enough?" he asked.

He seemed to be trying to read her to see if his brothers were irritating her. "I can take you home if you have."

"Oh, but she'll miss dessert if she goes," Simon piped up.

Gina grinned. "Can't have that. Besides, I want to help do the dishes. Sam told me that your dishwasher is broken," she said to Sanford.

Sanford smiled his approval of the young woman whom his friend Maizie had recruited at his request. "You're a guest. No menial labor for a guest."

"How about for a family member?" she asked, looking at Sam's father and wondering what he would say.

Sanford nodded, a big grin on his lips. "Sam, I do like this young woman. If nothing else," he went on, making eye contact with Gina, "I want you to keep her permanently employed at your clinic. If you recall, I gave you the start-up money to open it, so I do have some say in how it's run."

Sam raised his hands. "Fine with me, but ultimately, it's up to Gina."

Six sets of eyes turned to look at Gina, waiting for an answer.

Chapter Fifteen

Gina took her time answering. “Well, it does sound good to me, but why don’t we just take this one day at a time and see where this goes?” she suggested honestly. She couldn’t gauge how they all felt by their expressions, and she didn’t want to come on too strong. She felt she might ruin what could possibly be forming. “You might change your minds about this, and I wouldn’t want you to feel as if you had painted yourselves into a corner.”

Sanford stroked his chin. “Pretty, smart and cautious.” The smile he flashed Gina was close to blinding. “You know, you kind of remind me of the boys’ mother.”

It was hard for her not to beam at the man. Sam had told her how his father felt about the woman he had married. “That has to be the nicest thing anyone has ever said to me, Mr. Sterling,” she told him softly.

“Sanford,” Sam’s father reminded her. “Call me Sanford.”

But Gina shook her head. “Warm as this makes

me feel, this doesn't call for being on a first-name basis with you, sir. At least," she qualified, "not yet. Maybe somewhere down the line."

Sanford nodded, accepting her decision. "As you wish, my dear. Whatever makes you feel comfortable. But right now, washing dishes will be put on hold." His smile was bright, charming. "There will be servings of ice cream all around. Simon, if you would do the honors," he urged the son who was responsible for dinner that Sunday.

Gina frowned slightly. "I don't do well just sitting and waiting to be served," she began, wanting to at least take over serving dessert to the others.

To her surprise, Sam's father told her to "deal with it, my dear." His words were accompanied by a warm smile.

"You heard the man," Sam told her. "Sit."

Gina sighed and threw up her hands. This didn't make her happy, but she was not about to fight Sam and his father at every turn. "Sitting," she responded to both of the men.

"I do like a person who knows when to adjust to the situation." And then Sanford turned toward Simon. "That's your cue, son."

Rising, Simon went to the kitchen and returned with a half-gallon container of mint chip ice cream. Deftly, he scooped ice cream and distributed the bowls to his father, his brothers and Gina. Everyone had seconds.

* * *

It wasn't until hours later that Gina, Charlotte and Sam were finally back in Sam's car and on their way to the condo Gina was renting.

Sam glanced over at his assistant as they pulled away from the house where he and his brothers had grown up. She hadn't said much to him after telling his father and brothers how much she'd enjoyed meeting them.

"So how are you doing?" he asked.

"Just fine," she told him, then turned to look at Sam. "Why? Did you think I was going to disintegrate?"

"The thought did cross my mind," Sam confessed. "Five doses of Sterling men, then throw in our dad, and it all might be a little hard to take."

"I don't see why," she said. "From the way you talked, I was expecting to feel like I'd been dropped on an anthill after being dipped in honey. Instead, everyone was more entertaining and kind than the last person. Either you *really* exaggerated, or you all cast one hell of a spell over me." She grinned at him. "I'm kind of leaning toward explanation number one." And then she turned in her seat to look at the dog behind her. "How about you, Charlotte? Do you think that Dr. Sam exaggerated what his family was like to us?"

As if in agreement, the miniature collie barked.

Gina laughed. Turning back around, she told Sam,

"Charlotte said she didn't think you exaggerated. But then, we know my dog has been very partial to you ever since the day you sewed her up and saved her life. My guess is that Charlotte is going to be your faithful, extremely grateful shadow for the rest of your life—maybe even longer."

Sam smiled in response. "In all seriousness, that's why I got into this business. Animals are incredibly grateful and loyal. More so than a lot of people, in my opinion."

She was quiet for a moment. "That sounds to me as if you've had some bad experiences," Gina guessed.

"No, but Simon told me some stories about the clients he was dealing with that made me glad I haven't had time to garner any experiences of my own," Sam told her, stopping at a red light.

"That sounds like it could be very lonely," she said.

"No," he denied. He didn't have time to get lonely. "Just extremely busy. But that's the price I paid to start up my veterinary practice," he said philosophically. And happily, he thought, the pace hadn't let up yet.

"Well, I, for one, am glad you did," she told him with feeling.

"So," Sam said, deciding to change the subject, "what did you think of my family? You don't look worse for the wear, but for all I know, you could just be a really great actress."

Gina shook her head. "No acting. I honestly had a really great time. Your father and your brothers were all extremely funny, charming and very welcoming. I didn't expect to," she confessed, "but I had a really great time."

"Do you think," Sam began, broaching the subject slowly, "you would be willing to do this again?"

"Very willing," she said with what sounded like genuine sincerity. "I like seeing what actual family life could be like instead of just imagining it."

"Spoiler alert," Sam said, inclining his head toward her. "My dad and brothers behaved better than usual. There are times when they just sit at the table, communing with their dinners and counting the minutes before they can beat a hasty retreat."

Gina didn't seem fazed by this glimpse into his family's life. "That just means they're human. I wasn't expecting to meet a bunch of plaster saints."

"That's good," he responded. "Because if there's one thing they're not, it's saintly." He slanted a look in her direction. "So you really had a decent time? Because if you actually didn't, I want to apologize now."

"Yes, I really did have a decent time. *More* than decent," she emphasized. "There's absolutely nothing to apologize for. I enjoyed getting a glimpse into the world that made you you."

"So then you'll be in tomorrow?" he asked, glancing at her profile.

"Of course I'll be in tomorrow," she answered. "Where else would I be?" Then she added, "I consider myself one of the lucky ones."

Sam pulled up in front of her condo and turned off his car engine. "Come again?" he asked. Had he missed something? To his thinking, he was the lucky one.

"I'm getting paid to do what I always wanted to do. Work with animals," she clarified. "We have that in common."

"I guess we do." He had forgotten that she had told him that.

"I've got one more question for you," Gina said, unbuckling her seat belt but staying in her seat.

Sam wasn't aware that she had asked an initial question, but he went with it. "Go ahead."

"Do you cook as well as Simon does?" she asked curiously.

Genuinely tickled, Sam laughed. "At the risk of sounding immodest, better."

Gina seemed to roll that over in her head, then smiled. "That sounds promising."

"I'll make you something to eat sometime this week," Sam promised, not wanting her to think he was just bragging. He knew what he was capable of. He'd been the one who took care of his brothers when his mother became too ill to cook.

Gina waved at his offer. "Oh, you don't have to do

that just because I'm curious. You work hard enough as it is. I'll just take your word for it."

But Sam wasn't about to be put off that easily. "We'll get back to this," he promised, knowing how this debate would turn out if he kept going. "In the meantime, thanks for coming and putting up with everything. I'm serious."

"And thank you for a great time," she reciprocated. "I'm serious, too. Now, Charlotte and I need to beat a hasty retreat so you can go home and get some rest. You're going to need it. You've got a jam-packed schedule tomorrow," she told him.

Just as Sam turned his head toward her to tell her that the pleasure had been all his, Gina leaned in, saying, "Thank you."

She probably meant to brush her lips against his cheek. But because he had turned his head, their lips pressed against each other.

The contact generated a wave of electricity that was hard to describe. Or ignore. It zipped through Sam with speed, an incredible, unmatched power that was both startling and immensely seductive.

For a long moment, he felt like he had lost the ability to breathe like a normal person. Everything within him was tingling, as if a black-and-white world had suddenly been bathed in warm, magnificent rainbow colors.

He was kissing Gina.

Suddenly and unexpectedly.

This was definitely not what Sam had intended. He should be apologizing to her, not slipping his arms around her and pulling her to him. Why wasn't he drawing away and creating space between them?

In a minute, Sam told himself. *I'll do it in a minute. Just one minute longer, and then I'll pull back and apologize to her. After all, I didn't plan this. It just happened by accident. A very fortuitous accident.*

Summoning more strength than he would have thought necessary, he finally dropped his hands from her body. "I'm sorry. I didn't mean for that to happen," he told her, embarrassed.

"You didn't?" she asked.

He couldn't tell from her tone if she was being on the level, but his best bet was to go with sincerity. After all, she couldn't fault him for that. At least, he hoped not.

"No," he emphasized. "It was an accident, one of those flukes that happen sometimes. You turned your head just as I turned mine, and our lips somehow managed to make contact. I am really sorry if I offended you," he went on with feeling.

"You didn't," Gina told him. "Surprised me, yes, but offended me? No, you didn't do that. After all, you just said it was an accident. And I believe you." She paused for a moment, then asked him, "It was, wasn't it?"

Sam nodded his head a little too vigorously. "Yes."

But he was disappointed that she seemed to prefer that explanation over the fact that the kiss had stirred a tidal wave of incredible, heated feelings.

Chapter Sixteen

Gina and Charlotte stood on the doorstep of her condo, watching as Sam pulled away. Gina took in a deep breath, trying very hard to still her wildly beating pulse.

He would probably never know how close she had come to inviting him in for a drink. Gina had nothing on the premises that could be thought of as hard liquor, but there were definitely things in her cabinet that could give both of them more than just a pleasant buzz. Or at least her, she thought.

And if that happened, she would more than likely wind up dropping her defenses. Heaven knew that, right now, she was desperately trying everything in her power to keep those defenses raised and in place.

Just thinking about it had her heart fluttering. She had to admit that she had never felt this way about a man before. This was definitely a first. But Gina really liked her job, and she felt that the fastest way for her to lose it would be to invite Sam in and act on what she was feeling.

She didn't flatter herself that what she was experiencing right now was anything near mutual. She was going to have to keep a tight rein on her emotions and tread very, very carefully, Gina told herself.

Turning on her heel, she unlocked her door. Gina closed and locked it decisively behind her.

Sam kept his assistant and her pet in his rearview mirror for as long as he could. *That was close*, he thought.

But the odd thing was, he didn't know which outcome he was rooting for. Did he want to keep things businesslike between them or go with the intense feelings he was experiencing?

Okay, Sam did know what he was rooting for, but that could very well mean he might lose an incredibly gifted and able assistant. Every day that went by only served to show him how much he had gained by having Gina helping him in the clinic. Sam really didn't want to go back to steering through the choppy waters by himself if he could possibly avoid it.

Parking his car at the curb, Sam walked into his living quarters through the entrance to the clinic and called out, "I'm home, Rocky."

The German shepherd came barreling out of the room where she had been staying to greet him and all but knocked him down in her happiness to see him. Steadying himself, Sam laughed as he ran his hands along Rocky's fur.

"Are you glad to see me or is it the smell of the

spareribs that has you reacting this way?" he asked his pet.

Rocky was now all but inhaling the bag his father had packed up for him. He'd sent one of his other sons home with a serving of spareribs for his pets, too.

Sam shook his head as he watched Rocky. "You know, you'd get more out of it if you tried eating a little slower and actually *tasting* the meat," he chided the German shepherd.

But Rocky went through the spareribs like a house on fire.

"Okay, have it your way. Me, I'm going to bed," he told her.

Pausing only long enough to refill her bowl with water, Sam went up to his room. He had to force himself to put one foot in front of the other and strip off his shirt and his shoes for bed. He came close to just falling on top of his mattress fully clothed and completely devoid of energy. He hadn't realized he was this exhausted until the allure of sleep pulled him in.

It took him less than five minutes to fall into a deep, dreamless sleep.

The following week was practically a repeat of the previous one. Different pets came in to be treated, but by and large there was nothing new or earth-shattering on the agenda.

Not until Gina took an emergency phone call from

a woman who asked, "What sort of pets does Dr. Sterling treat?"

"The usual ones," Gina answered. "Dogs, cats, an assortment of birds." She thought for a moment, thinking of the parade of pets that had been brought into the office in the last couple of weeks. "Also lizards and hamsters."

"Anything else?" the woman asked, sounding a little uncertain.

"It might be simpler if you tell me what animal you're thinking of bringing in," Gina told her.

The caller took in a deep breath before she finally said, "My horse isn't doing well."

Gina was caught off guard. "Your horse?" she repeated, stunned. She had to admit that this was a pet she hadn't been expecting. "I'm going to have to check with Dr. Sterling about that. I'm new here, and so far, I haven't seen any horses on the schedule." Gina congratulated herself for getting those words out without stumbling. "Can you hold on for a moment?"

The woman sounded rather beside herself as she answered, "Yes, I'll hold on."

This wasn't a joke, Gina decided. Putting the woman on hold, Gina went to knock lightly on the door to the secondary exam room. Then she opened the door cautiously and peeked in.

Sam raised his eyes from the poodle he was examining, a silent query.

"I have a rather distraught woman on the phone asking if you examine horses," Gina told him.

"In an emergency, if she can't get an equine veterinarian to come by and examine it, I can do it," Sam told her. "Get all the details you can and tell her we can come by last thing today." He paused, as if realizing he was taking something for granted. "You are available, right?"

Gina smiled as she nodded her head. "Yes, I'm available," she assured him. Then, so that he didn't misunderstand her meaning, she added, "To accompany you to the ranch." Withdrawing from the room, she closed the door behind her.

Finished with the clinic's scheduled patients for the day, they had driven to an old ranch on the edge of town. Sam had easily diagnosed the stallion and applied a relatively simple solution, bringing a relieved smile from the horse's owner, Molly Sanders.

"Flicka was a gift from my father. My father passed away last fall, and the horse is my last connection to him," Molly confessed. "I'd like to keep Flicka alive as long as I possibly can."

"Well, from everything I can see, once we get this infection under control, Flicka gives every indication of being able to live a long, healthy life," Sam told her. Other than his current problem, Flicka was an impressive piece of horseflesh.

An hour later, Sam and Gina left Molly fairly beaming as they drove away from the ranch and headed back to Aurora.

Gina had offered to drive them back to the clinic, thinking that Sam must be fairly tired. But when she suggested it, he turned her down.

"This is still a fairly unknown area to you, and the darkness here isn't your friend. It's easy to get lost, so I'll drive us back to the clinic—but thanks for the offer," Sam added.

Knowing it was useless to argue, Gina leaned back against her seat. "Dogs, cats, birds, reptiles, hamsters and now horses. You certainly are versatile," Gina commented. "Are there any animals you don't know how to treat?" She could hear the admiration echoing in her own voice.

"I sincerely hope not." And then he smiled at her before looking back at the road. "Maybe a dinosaur."

"Not a problem. Those aren't around anymore except in the movies," Gina reminded him.

"Well then, I guess the answer to your question is a resounding no," Sam told her with a wide grin.

Gina laughed softly. "Brilliant, capable and modest, too," she teased. "Is there no end to your attributes, Doctor?"

His eyes met hers, then went back to watching the road. "I don't know. I guess that remains to be seen," he told her with an easy smile that even in the darkness shot straight into her nervous system, making it quiver.

Twenty minutes later, Sam pulled up in front of the clinic. “You put in a really long day today,” he said. It sounded like a compliment.

“So did you,” Gina pointed out.

“I should. I’m the vet and this is my clinic,” he said.

“That doesn’t mean you need to do this by yourself. I’m here to help any way I can,” she reminded him.

Instead of arguing, he just shook his head as if in wonder. “I don’t know how I ever managed to run this place without you.”

“Now you’re just flattering me,” she said.

“No,” he denied, looking at her. “I am just telling you the truth.”

Gina raised a quizzical eyebrow, her mouth curving in amusement. She didn’t believe the man for a moment. She couldn’t allow herself to. “Really?” she challenged.

“Really,” Sam told her without even a hint of wavering.

Gina began to open the car door. “Let me go collect Charlotte, and we’ll be out of your hair as quickly as possible.”

But Sam rounded the hood of his vehicle to help her out—not that she needed it.

Gina smiled up at him. “You don’t need to go out of your way like that, Doctor. I am perfectly capable of getting out of the car all on my own.”

"I know that," he said. "This is just my way of saying thank you for all your help."

"You're paying me for doing that," Gina reminded him.

"There's help, and then there's help," he said, changing his tone between the two words. "And after what I've been through in getting my clinic on its feet, I've learned not to take a single thing for granted."

Gina nodded seriously. "I don't, either." But even still, right now, she found herself responding to the way Sam was treating her. His treatment could change eventually, or possibly abruptly, but so far, it hadn't and gave no indication that it would anytime soon. If anything, it only seemed to be getting better.

This was what she got for leading a solitary life, Gina told herself. If she had gotten involved with men on any regular basis, she wouldn't be melting like this at any display of kindness.

No, she corrected herself. It wasn't that she had been living a solitary life. She just hadn't lit up inside before when someone paid attention to her. Up until now, she hadn't had time for it. It wasn't until Sam that Gina began to feel as if she was actually lighting up inside.

Over and over again, she thought with a smile that she managed to hide—or at least she thought she did.

"Okay, let's show Charlotte that you're here to take her home," Sam said, unlocking the clinic's door.

The moment he did, they could hear the miniature collie's agitated barking.

"Looks like someone knows that her mom's here to pick her up," Sam commented with a grin.

"There are those canine instincts again," Gina marveled as she made her way to the room where Charlotte was playing with Rocky.

When Gina and Sam walked in, all furry activity stopped abruptly as two pairs of eyes turned toward the humans. Charlotte instantly barked a happy greeting at her mistress, leaping up excitedly and dancing around on her hind legs.

Delighted, both Gina and Sam began to laugh wholeheartedly.

Chapter Seventeen

It just kept getting better and better.

With each day that passed, Gina felt she had definitely made the right decision to help Sam with his clinic. Without being conceited, she felt that she was the right person for this job.

Actually, at this point it wasn't just a job. Gina felt as if working in Sam's shadow was more of a vocation, a calling. It was what she had always been meant to do. Up until now, she had held down jobs merely to keep body and soul together so she could eat and pay rent. If even one of those jobs had been remotely satisfying, she wouldn't have constantly been busy looking for the next job.

Since she had begun working at the clinic, she was no longer looking. She had found her rightful place in the scheme of things.

And that was also applicable, in no small way, not just to what she was doing, but how she felt about what she was doing. That went for the animals she was working with as well as the veterinarian she was working beside. He never asked anything of her that he didn't ask of himself; that went for the hours she put in as well.

Gina had to constantly remind herself not to get too carried away. She knew that she very easily could with no effort—in less than the blink of an eye, she thought, her mouth curving.

"Something funny?" Sam asked as he paused at her desk on his way into the second exam room. A husky and his master were waiting to see him. These days, Sam was able to work his way through an afternoon's patients at less than an exhausting pace.

"No," Gina replied innocently.

Sam's eyes narrowed. "You're grinning."

She maintained her innocent expression and shrugged. "I'm just happy, I guess."

Sam didn't tell Gina he was happy to hear her response, but he really didn't need to get a confirmation from her about how she felt.

Four Sundays had gone by, and he had invited her to four Sunday dinners, and she had shown up to all of them. It had gotten to the point that not only did he look forward to the relaxed atmosphere at these dinners, but he realized that his father and brothers looked forward to seeing Gina—which was a great feeling.

Sam hung back for a moment longer before going to Room Two. "Does that mean that you'll be coming to Sunday dinner again? I'm asking," he explained quickly, "because my dad asked me if you would be there."

"Your dad's a very sweet man," Gina said with enthusiasm. "You know, I don't understand why he never got married again."

"The torch that my dad's carrying for my mom is just too heavy and too bright for him to consider someone else. I don't think anyone would ever be able to get him to move past it," Sam said.

She smiled at him. "You know, that really sounds like a challenge."

Sam read between the lines and immediately tried to veto what she must be thinking. "Oh, no, please don't try to play matchmaker where my father's concerned." From the way Gina's smile widened, he knew he had guessed correctly.

"Why not?" she asked innocently. "Don't you want to see your father happy?"

"Of course I want to see him happy. What I don't want to see is my old man handing my head to me. Look, we'll talk about this later," he told her. "I've got a patient to see in Room Two right now, but I'll get back to this after hours if you want to talk further."

Gina inclined her head. "Oh, absolutely."

She didn't get to talk to Sam again until the clinic's front door was finally locked for the day.

"Isn't your family tired of seeing me at the dinner table with them?" she asked him. When he raised his eyebrows, she explained, "I really don't want to wear out my welcome."

"You're kidding, right?" he asked. "You've made Sunday dinners something for the rest of us to look forward to."

Gina shook her head. "You don't have to lie to spare my feelings."

He looked at her, clearly surprised. "I'm not lying. And those aren't just my sentiments. I'm telling you what my father and brothers have expressed. It seems like you've cast quite a spell over all of them—no easy feat, I don't mind telling you."

She wasn't sure how he actually meant that, or even *if* he meant that. "That wasn't my intention, Sam."

"Maybe not," he allowed, "but it still happened. And it's not a bad thing. This is one of those rare times that my whole family seems to be in complete agreement."

"Okay, now you're just pulling my leg," Gina told him.

"No, I'm not." *Although the prospect of that is definitely not off-putting*, he couldn't help thinking, his eyes skimming along the outline of her body. He found his appetite growing to greater proportions and unbelievable heights. For just a second, their eyes met and locked.

Gina felt a warm surge traveling through her, touching every single part of her body. It was happening again, she thought. She could feel desire growing, taking possession of her. She needed to be on her way, or she was going to wind up just melting right here on the spot.

"I think it's time for me to take Charlotte home," she told him.

Sam knew he should step out of Gina's way, even encourage her to take her pet and be on her way. But the words telling her to go refused to leave his lips.

And then he thought of something.

"Tell you what. Why don't I make you and Charlotte dinner?" Sam suggested, bending to pet the miniature collie's head.

Gina didn't think that was a very good idea, but she didn't want to tell him that. She went with logic instead. "Well, for one thing, you have to be tired. You put in as long a day as I did."

"Actually, cooking relaxes me," he told her.

She waved her hand, not believing him. "How is that possible? Cooking always makes me feel uptight."

Sam shrugged. "Different strokes for different folks, I guess. So, about dinner. Are you game?"

Gina nodded. "I'm game, but I'm also going to feel pretty guilty, putting you out like this."

"You're not putting me out," he insisted. "I wouldn't have suggested it otherwise." He thought for a moment. "Would you feel better if you assisted me in this venture?" he asked, a smile curving his mouth.

"Yes, I would," she answered.

"Okay, consider yourself my assistant in this as well," Sam told her. "It's like extending our work relationship to another level." His smile widened. "Does that work for you?"

Well, she certainly couldn't just walk out on him now, Gina thought. So she nodded her head and said, "Yes, it does."

"I'm glad." Sam grinned again. "I've never cooked with an assistant before." His eyes met hers. "This should be an interesting experience."

Interesting wasn't the word she would have used, but Gina supposed that in a pinch it would do. "Just tell me what you want me to do, and I'll do it," she told him.

From the expression on his face, she realized how that sounded.

Clearing her throat, Gina said in a deeper voice, "You know what I mean."

Sam nodded. "Sadly," he told her, "I know exactly what you mean. Okay, let's get to work." He led the way to his kitchen.

The refrigerator appeared to be totally stocked. Gina remembered how it had looked just the other morning when he invited her to have some orange juice.

"Do you have elves?" she asked him whimsically, gesturing at the fridge.

Sam laughed. "No, but I do have a brother who

knows how to shop and fill a refrigerator. And he owes me a favor."

"Well, in some circles, that's even better than elves," she joked.

"There were times growing up when I would have rather had the elves," he told her seriously. Sam opened the refrigerator door wide. "Okay," he said, waving a hand, "what's your pleasure?"

Gina shrugged. It really made no difference to her. "I'm fairly easy to please. You pick."

He decided to try to learn a few things about her tastes. "How do you feel about pork chops?"

That was easy. She had liked those ever since she was a little girl. "I like them breaded and fried," she answered.

"I do, too." He glanced over at Rocky and Charlotte, who appeared very interested in what was going on. "And I guarantee that the dogs will be happy to eat the leftovers."

Gina looked at him. "What makes you think there're going to be leftovers?" she asked innocently. "I think you know by now that I'm not one of those people who just nibble delicately."

"Is there a reason for that? Other than good cooking, I mean," he asked.

"Food was hard to come by when I was growing up. At the risk of sounding as if I stuff myself, I learned to appreciate every morsel that finds its way to my plate," she said. "I thought you might have picked up on that these last few weeks."

"I just thought you were trying not to insult my brothers' cooking," he confessed.

"Well, there's that, too," Gina allowed with a smile. "But if that were the case, I would have just nibbled the way you anticipated. But at your father's table, there has never been any need to pretend. So far, your brothers are excellent cooks. When is it going to be your turn?" she asked.

"As a matter of fact, my turn is this Sunday," he told her.

"Fantastic," she exclaimed. She pretended to be calm as she asked, "Am I allowed to help you this Sunday, or does this have to be a solo venture?"

"Well, my brothers didn't have anyone working with them, but then, they don't have anyone in their lives who *can* cook," he emphasized.

She nodded and stepped up to work beside him, doing her best not to get in his way at the same time. "So I can consider this a rehearsal for Sunday," she told him, reaching for the potatoes he put out for her to peel and dice.

"Only if you want to—you're not required to help," he insisted. "You can just be a guest and enjoy yourself. No one will think any less of you."

"Maybe not, but I will," she told him. "I told you that first Sunday, I don't like being a sponge."

"Then I guess it's settled," Sam concluded. "You'll be my assistant there, too."

Gina smiled at him. "Happy to comply, Doctor."

Chapter Eighteen

Much to Sam's surprise and pleasure, he and Gina worked as well together in the kitchen as they did in the clinic. Once he told her what he was planning to prepare, Gina seemed to instinctively anticipate his every move in the kitchen, just as she had begun to do at the clinic. Dinner was ready in record time, and they were both rather pleased with the end result.

"I'll do the dishes," Gina announced once they had finished eating.

"The dishwasher will do the dishes," Sam told her pointedly.

"You had it fixed?" she asked, surprised. He had mentioned the other day that the dishwasher was broken.

"*I* fixed it," he corrected her. Sam prided himself on being able to repair a number of things that would cause the average person to call in a repair person.

Gina looked rather impressed. "I guess you're pretty handy."

Sam smiled. "I'd like to think so."

"Still," Gina said, "I feel that the dishes are cleaner

if I'm the one washing them instead of a machine." She turned her back to him to run hot, sudsy water in the sink.

"You really don't have to do that," Sam told her, coming up behind her and attempting to take a dish out of her hands. "Sit back for once. You already have enough to do."

Gina refused to let go. "Oh, and you don't?"

"I already told you, the clinic is my practice and my responsibility," Sam reminded her.

"Maybe I want to start up my own practice," she challenged, turning around to face him.

The problem was that she turned in what amounted to be the circle of his arms, her mouth incredibly close to his. The warmth of his breath traveling over her face startled her. Her lips were all but brushing against his.

Her heart leaped as she remembered the first time they had been in this situation. When she had moved to kiss his cheek and wound up kissing his mouth instead. Since that time, she had found herself longing for a repeat performance. A longer, more sensual repeat performance.

And then suddenly, it was happening.

Sam framed her face with his hands and brought his mouth down to hers. This wasn't just a light meeting of their lips only to pull back. This time Gina could feel the passion hiding just beneath the surface. Passion that spoke to something within her, and though she knew she should pull away, she really, really didn't want to.

So she didn't.

Instead, her arms went around his neck, and she closed the gap between them, drawing Sam in. Before she really even knew what was happening, she felt her body pressed achingly close to his. She had absolutely no desire for any sort of separation between them. Her pulse throbbed, racing madly throughout her entire body.

"This shouldn't be happening," Sam told her. But there was no conviction in his voice.

"I know," she answered, but did nothing to create even the smallest amount of space between them.

He drew his head back just for a moment, his eyes searching hers. He must have found the answer he needed because he brought his mouth back down to hers with even more passion.

Sam picked her up in his arms and carried her to the one bedroom downstairs. Pushing the door open with his shoulder, he set her down so her feet touched the floor. Then he drew back again to look at her as well as to give her an option. This was all new and he didn't want to push ahead and presume anything.

"If this is going too fast for you or if you want to stop, all you need to do is just say so," he said.

"And you'll stop? Just like that?" she questioned, surprised.

"Well, it wouldn't be 'just like that,'" Sam told her.

"But I definitely don't want to do anything that you don't want to do or that makes you uncomfortable. This won't have a prayer of working if it's just one-sided."

"A prayer of *working*," she echoed, emphasizing all the word implied. "Does that mean you want to do this beyond tonight?"

The look he gave her could have easily melted an entire mountain of snow. "Hell yes," he told her in no uncertain terms.

That was all she wanted to hear. Yes, she knew that men lied to women in intimate situations. She also knew that the reverse could be true. This time, when Gina brought her lips to his, she held nothing back, lighting a bonfire within her that heretofore had no equal.

Breathing hard, Sam drew back one last time. "Is that a yes?" he asked.

Frustration all but echoed in Gina's voice. "If I have to answer that—" she began.

Gina didn't get a chance to finish. Or to even breathe normally. The rest of what she was about to say was submerged in a whirlwind of passion that captured them both.

They fell onto the bed, bodies entwined with one another as each rained kisses on the other's face and any skin they were able to access.

Gina dragged Sam's shirt off his shoulders and arms, her fingers skimming along his bare skin, her lips passionately anointing the areas being exposed.

Sam returned the favor, mimicking her movements and fanning the bonfire within her. Bit by bit, clothing disappeared, until they were both dressed only in the other's warm gaze and hot touch.

The little voice in her head that had initially shouted "Stop!" slowly faded to a soft whisper and then nothingness. It was replaced by a yearning that threatened to finally consume her. Her body curled up and around his, continuing to build the fire within her.

So this was what it was like, Sam thought, what he had heard people talking about and praising for years. Until now, he had just shrugged his shoulders, telling himself that if this wild, elusive thing called love was meant to happen, it *would* happen, and he left it at that. He certainly hadn't thought it could grow to these extremes.

Not until Gina had come his way. Suddenly things began happening inside of him. His attention was being drawn away from the events of his day-to-day life and from his time-consuming, nonstop practice. Now there was something beyond that, Sam realized, and that thought did not leave him feeling unhappy.

Gina twisted and turned, eager for Sam's touch. Each pass of his hand generated more and more heat along her skin and inside of her, her hunger growing ravenous.

Suddenly, Sam moved so that his body was directly over hers, heat emanating from him. He linked his hands with hers, and as their eyes met and held, he coaxed her legs apart with his knee and then entered her, moving his hips with an ever-growing urgency as their bodies finally became one.

The explosion finally came, the euphoria of it nearly consuming them as it traveled urgently through their entire bodies. They clung to one another, absorbing the fierce shudder that vibrated through them until it finally settled down, leaving a warm feeling behind.

Sam raised his head to look at her. "Wow." Kissing her forehead softly, he repeated, "Wow."

Gina was having a great deal of difficulty stilling her pounding pulse. Finally, she was able to ask, "So this is over?"

Cocking his head, Sam asked, "Come again?"

"You just kissed my forehead like a big brother, so I just wanted to know if that's your way of saying that this is now over." She was only a little serious, but there was indeed a part of her that was afraid that was what it meant.

"No, it's my way of saying that you exhausted me beyond all comprehension and this is all I have the energy to do," Sam told her. "I'm just waiting for my energy to come back, and then we can pick up where we left off."

She laughed softly. "You're going to have a very long wait. You really drained me, too."

"At least that feeling is mutual," he said. "I guess that means we're well suited for one another." Sam smiled. "I'm also guessing that I'm not supposed to say that."

She eyed him quizzically. "Why not?"

"Well, it takes the mystery out of things," he told her.

"I wasn't aware that mystery was called for in this case," Gina said innocently.

"According to authorities on these matters, mystery is what helps propel things along between two lovers," Sam told her.

"Do you really believe that?" she asked.

Sam shook his head. "Just telling you the popular theory. I don't believe in playing games. But then, and this might not be a good thing to admit, either," he allowed, "I've never really had a steady girlfriend. I never learned all the games that need to be played in a relationship."

Gina moved so that her body curled into his again. "I was always too busy holding body and soul together to get involved in all those so-called games." She raised herself on her elbow to look at him. "For the record, I don't believe in playing games, either."

Sam pulled her down to him, fanning the flames between them to new heights again. He grinned at her. "I just believe in going with the truth."

"Very alluring and sexy. Me, too." Gina sealed her lips to his, starting their erotic dance all over again.

Chapter Nineteen

They made love three times that night. Which accounted for the extremely happy glow Gina felt within her the following morning.

Even so, as the days went by, Gina knew she shouldn't attach too much attention to what she was experiencing or even become the slightest bit used to it. She had heard too many stories about people feeling undying love, only for it to do just that: die, leaving people utterly bereft and extremely empty inside, like everything had just been ripped out.

She didn't want to go through that in any way and was completely determined not to. She attempted to construct an impenetrable wall around herself in order to remain invulnerable from anything to do with Sam. She was already responding way too much, way too strongly to the man's charms.

And he really *was* charming.

Gina slanted a glance in Sam's direction in the clinic one morning. It was definitely not easy to stay strong. They had made love a number of times, both before and after they had spent a traditional Sunday dinner with Sam's family. He made her heart smile with so very little effort.

Going over the paperwork from his latest patient, Gina struggled not to stare at Sam as he spoke to the owner. It was certainly hard not to give in when every thought in her head revolved around the veterinarian.

Such as this Pekingese, aptly named Furball, who had come in with a pronounced limp. A limp that she seemed to have acquired with no sign of outward injury.

"But there *has* to be a reason," Mrs. Martin insisted, looking as if she was close to bursting into tears.

Sam took a breath. He would have thought that the reason was self-evident. "Oh, I'm afraid there is."

Pulling her shoulders back, Mrs. Martin braced herself with a frown. "I don't like the way that sounds, Dr. Sterling."

"I'm afraid that to rectify this particular situation, it's going to take a lot of discipline on your part, Mrs. Martin," Sam told her.

The woman pulled her shoulders back even farther, looking every inch a soldier ready to go into battle for a beloved cause. "Tell me," she urged. "I can handle it."

Sam had his doubts about that being even remotely true. This whole situation could have been avoided if Mrs. Martin had exhibited the slightest bit of self-control and not grossly overfed her Pekingese at every turn.

"Furball is limping like that," he told her, "because she is way too heavy. You're a pushover, and you've fed her too much. She looks up at you with those great big, sad brown eyes, begging for treats, and you give in and toss food at her just to placate her." Sam didn't mean to criticize, but he had to tell her the way he saw things.

"But Furball looks so terribly pathetic when she's hungry," Mrs. Martin said, looking concerned that she was to blame for her beloved pet's weight. Perhaps she thought her explanation was good enough to absolve her of blame.

"You have to understand that Furball is a very bright dog. She has learned how to use looking pathetic to get what she wants," Sam told Mrs. Martin.

The dog's owner appeared stricken.

Gina turned away from her desk. The expression on Mrs. Martin's face tore at her heart. The woman looked extremely guilty. "Mrs. Martin, if Furball was your child instead of your pet, would you allow her to overeat like that because she stuck out her lower lip and pouted at you?" Gina asked in a kindly voice. She was sympathetic for what the woman had to be going through.

"No, of course not," Mrs. Martin answered with pronounced feeling.

"Then should you allow your dog to do that sort of thing?" Gina asked logically.

Mrs. Martin opened her mouth defensively, then

closed it again, clearly stumped. "No, of course not," she finally answered.

"And why is that?" Gina asked, aware that Sam was watching her. When Mrs. Martin didn't say anything, Gina said, "It's because you love Furball, right? Do you love her any less than if she were your child?" Gina knew from Mrs. Martin's file that, for all intents and purposes, she regarded Furball as her child.

"No, of course not," the woman protested adamantly.

"Well, you're going to have to remain very strong when she turns those big, sad eyes to look at you," Gina told her. "Think about the good you are doing by staying so strong."

She glanced toward Sam to see if she had overstepped. His approving smile and the way he nodded at her let her release the breath she had been holding. She hadn't made a mistake. Not only that, but Sam didn't resent her butting into his practice. She was just trying to make the woman realize what Sam was attempting to convey about her pet.

"I am going to write a prescription for something you can give Furball that will fill her up so she doesn't feel hungry," Sam said to Mrs. Martin. "If Furball feels full, she's not going to haunt your every step, trying to get you to give her treats. They're pretty straightforward when it comes to their appetites. This is all going to take a little while," Sam predicted, "but she will lose the weight and stop limping when she loses that extra weight."

Mrs. Martin had tears in her eyes as she looked down at her pet. "Really?"

Sam nodded. "Really," he told the woman with compassion.

She drew Furball onto her lap, although it obviously was not easy for the woman, and hugged the dog to her. "I don't know how to thank you, Dr. Sterling," she told Sam and then looked at Gina as well, including her in her gratitude.

"Just stick to your promise and don't overfeed Furball," Sam advised. "And that will be thanks enough for us."

Mrs. Martin nodded. "Oh, I won't overfeed her," she promised. "I've definitely learned my lesson."

"Remember," Sam told her, "what you perceive as kindness is actually harming the poor thing. Overeating puts a strain on Furball's heart, and you don't want to be responsible for doing that, do you?"

"No, of course not," Mrs. Martin cried with more than a little feeling.

"Glad to hear that. Gina, print up a copy of that special diet plan for Mrs. Martin to use when she's feeding Furball," Sam said.

"Right away, Dr. Sterling," Gina told him, going over to the filing cabinet. She retrieved the diet plan that Sam had asked her for and took it over to the copy machine. After quickly running off the pages,

Gina placed them in a folder and handed it to Mrs. Martin. "There you go," Gina announced.

Mrs. Martin glanced at the two pages, absorbing the information.

"If you have any questions," Sam said, "please don't hesitate to call me. And here," he said, writing on his prescription pad and tearing off a page, "is that prescription I mentioned. There's a phone number where you can reach me 24/7."

"And if I call it, you'll answer?" Mrs. Martin asked skeptically.

Sam smiled at the woman, petting Furball's head gently. "Yes, that's the deal."

Gina could almost read the woman's mind. "Dr. Sterling is quite serious. The first time I met him was when I brought my own dog to him. Charlotte had been attacked by a pit bull, and Dr. Sterling was kind enough to sew her up."

Mrs. Martin looked stunned. "Is this true?" she asked Sam.

He nodded. "Oh, it's true, all right. What Gina neglected to tell you is that this all took place at three o'clock in the morning."

"You really are one of the good ones, Dr. Sterling," Mrs. Martin told him.

Gina smiled. "He really is. Instead of reading me the riot act that I hadn't been careful with Charlotte when I realized there was a pit bull in the street, he took care of my dog and then later hired me as his assistant," she told Mrs. Martin proudly. "I guarantee that you will never find a better animal doctor for your pet."

"I am beginning to realize that," Mrs. Martin agreed. "I plan on telling all my friends. I belong to an exclusive club with a great many animal owners in its ranks. Once I finish singing your praises, you're going to have more business than you can possibly handle, Dr. Sterling."

"The doctor is already at maximum capacity," Gina said to the woman.

"Then I guess I'm lucky he was able to shoehorn me in," Mrs. Martin said with a gleeful smile. "And I intend to tell all my friends about him so he can pick and choose his clientele."

Gina glanced at Sam. She knew he was loyal to his original patients. She just hoped he wouldn't wear himself out. She knew firsthand that he had trouble turning people away.

"You know," Gina said once Mrs. Martin and Furball had left the clinic, "you might be forced to take on a partner."

"We can handle the extra business," he told her.

"We?" she questioned. "I'm not a veterinarian."

"No, but you're my assistant—and what you don't know, I can certainly train you so that you do," Sam predicted.

That sounded really promising, Gina couldn't help thinking.

Chapter Twenty

Gina found herself looking forward to Sundays a great deal. Sam, his four brothers and his father might not actually be her family, but she was beginning to think of them in that light. If she were given the option of selecting a family from scratch, the Sterlings were definitely the ones she would choose every time.

Except for Sam, she thought.

The feelings she was experiencing for the veterinarian were definitely not platonic. It might be rather premature for her to say, or even think, but she was beginning to believe that she was falling in love with the man.

She had never felt anything even close to this sort of emotion before, just as she had never felt remotely close to being part of a large family before Sam's father and brothers came into her life. This was all completely new to her, but exceedingly welcome.

Gina liked the warm feeling she experienced when she and Sam walked into his father's house and were greeted by his family. She had to admit that growing up she had felt almost like an inconvenience to her mother, like someone who'd gotten in the way of her mother doing something else with her time and her money.

But from the very first moment she met the Sterlings, she had felt welcomed by them.

"Hello, Sam, Gina," his father called out when they walked in. He paused, looking at Gina with an exceptionally bright smile. "You're looking particularly lovely today, my dear."

Sam arched an eyebrow at his father. "Dad, behave yourself," he warned.

"Gina knows I don't mean anything by it, don't you, Gina?" Sanford asked. "I'm assuming you told her that your mother was the only woman for me ever." He glanced between them. "I am really hoping that you two have the good fortune to experience something like that yourselves. Take it from me—there is no better feeling than loving someone as intensely as your mother and I loved one another."

Sanford turned toward the rest of his sons, who were already seated around the dinner table. "That goes for the rest of you as well."

"We know, Dad. Believe me, we know," Sebastian told his father with more than a little feeling.

"I didn't mean to insinuate that you don't," Sanford said. Then, jerking his thumb at Simon, he told Gina, "Simon was in charge of preparing the family dinner today. So, what did you decide to grace us with today?" he asked his son.

"Why don't you wait until I put it on the table for you?" Simon suggested.

"Ah, a surprise," Gina guessed, smiling at the solemn man.

Sean rolled his eyes. "That's what we're all afraid of," he confided to her in a stage whisper accompanied by a broad wink.

Gina felt it was up to her to come to Simon's defense, even if she hadn't sampled what the man was prepared to serve. "That wasn't very nice, Sean."

"Hey," Sean protested. "Simon's my brother. There's no law that says I have to be nice to him," he said to the woman whom he and the rest of his brothers thought of not just as Sam's assistant, but as Sam's girlfriend as well.

"Boys, boys, boys, settle down," Sanford told his sons sternly. "We have company. Remember to behave yourselves, please."

Gina looked a little disappointed. "I would think that by now you wouldn't think of me as company."

"She's right, Dad," Sam said. "Gina's not company anymore. She's morphed into family."

Sanford's face lit up. "Is there something you want to tell us, Sam?" he asked, his voice trailing off hopefully.

Sam shrugged. "Just that she's been here so much, she should think of this as her second home."

Gina silently told her pulse to go back to beating normally. There was no reason for it to speed up to double time. Yes, she and Sam had made love, glorious love, a number of times now, but that kind of thing happened between a man and a woman who clicked. It didn't necessarily mean anything serious or permanent.

It certainly didn't necessarily mean what she wanted it to mean.

With effort, Gina pulled her lips back into a smile, although she had to admit that she was forcing herself to appear happy in front of Sam and the others. She wanted Sam to believe that she didn't need this to be anything more than a passing, pleasant experience. She couldn't wait for dinner to be on the table so that they could get to the business of eating.

When it was finally served, it turned out to be a tasty rendition of Hungarian goulash. She looked at Simon with unabashed surprise. "This is very good," she told him.

"You sound as if you didn't expect it to be," Simon observed somewhat defensively.

"You're a divorce lawyer," she pointed out. "Most lawyers go out to eat a lot. They don't bother preparing things for themselves."

"They do if they're my sons," Sanford told her proudly. "Eating out can get really expensive. This way they understand how to save their money for the important things. Being frugal is the very first lesson I taught each one of my sons. That's something they're not about to forget and can put to good use."

"And that is a very valuable lesson," Gina agreed.

Sanford smiled at her, feeling extremely satisfied with himself for being instrumental in arranging for Gina and Sam to initially get together. He glanced at Sam and said, "Looks like your assistant gets me."

Gina beamed at the family patriarch. "Thank you. I consider that to be a compliment, coming from you, Mr. Sterling. And yes, I do."

"Bright and polite. What more can a man ask for?" Sanford asked Sam.

Gina grinned. "A lot of things, more than likely, but that would be a good start for a relationship."

Sanford winked at her as if they were sharing a secret. "It would indeed. But please, call me Sanford, not Mr. Sterling," he said, repeating the request he had made the first time they met. He put his hand on top of hers, as if about to share a secret. "My wife would have really liked you," he told her.

He turned toward Sam. Sam had been old enough when Shirley passed to form an opinion about what her reaction would be now to someone like Gina. "What do you think, Sam? Think your mother would have liked Gina?"

Sam inclined his head. "You know, she would have. I think you're right about that, Dad."

"Thank you, Mr. Sterling," Gina said, nodding at Sam's father. "I am exceedingly flattered by your comment."

Sanford slanted a glance toward his oldest son.

Sam looked rather pleased with what Gina had said. He really, *really* wanted to tell Sam that he was the one responsible for Gina being in his life, that he had found Gina and was behind her coming to Sam's clinic. He hadn't been instrumental in having her pet injured, of course, but he was behind her knowing about Sam's services. Sanford had also had a friend of his plant Sam's name and qualifications in Gina's head while she was trying to find a job to her liking. Luckily, she had known about Sam when her dog needed it the most. Funny how things turned out, Sanford thought.

But he knew that he could never say anything. For one thing, because this was working out so well, he wanted to have Maizie suggest another suitable young lady for one of his other sons. He intended to "plant" the appropriate son's name with the appropriate young lady that she provided him. Next up, Sanford thought, would be Simon. His divorce-lawyer son really needed a push in the right direction. Simon had become jaded to the subject of marriage, thanks to what he did for a living.

Once Sam and Gina were all wrapped up, Sanford intended to turn to Maizie again for help finding a match. He would hope that lightning could strike twice.

Out of the corner of his eye, Sanford saw Gina rising from the table. "Are you going somewhere, my dear?" he asked her, curious.

"I thought I'd take care of the dishes," she told him.

She felt good about being instrumental in taking care of cleanup.

"Regardless, Gina, you are to remain seated. Scott, you can take care of the dishes." He saw that his third son was about to protest, but he interrupted him. "Consider it a dry run for next Sunday."

"Dad, I've been doing this forever. I don't need a dry run," Scott protested.

"When you walk through that door, Scott, I would appreciate it if you left that argumentative side of you outside," his father told him seriously.

"Well, that went well," Gina said as she and Sam drove away from the house where he had grown up several hours later.

"If you mean that my father seems pretty taken with you, I totally agree," Sam told her. "Don't forget, until you appeared at our table, the only female who ever took a seat at our dinner table was Randi—and once we were grown, she stopped making regular appearances at Sunday dinner."

"From everything you tell me about her, Randi sounds like a pretty terrific person. Will I ever get to meet her?" Gina asked.

Sam glanced at her, a thoughtful expression on his face. "Would you want to?"

"Oh, very much," she told him enthusiastically. "After all, she helped raise you and your brothers, didn't she?"

Randi had done a great deal more than just raise them, Sam thought. The woman helped forge their paths through childhood and into adulthood. "Yes, she did," Sam told her.

"Well, she sounds like a pretty amazing lady to me," Gina said.

Sam smiled, remembering certain things from his own childhood. "Oh, she really is."

"Then I would really love to meet her," Gina told him.

"Okay, I'll run it by Dad," Sam told her.

Gina settled back in her seat. "You do that."

There was no missing her smile, Sam thought, feeling its effects and definitely enjoying it.

Chapter Twenty-One

After conducting extensive interviews with an aching heart, Sanford had chosen Randi Wayne to be his housekeeper and his sons' nanny because of her maternal and loving nature. While he was not looking for a replacement for his wife, he was searching for someone who could care for his sons and help them through this extremely difficult time.

He didn't come right out and tell Randi that. He wanted to see how she would work out before making her think that he was awarding her the position because of the way she came across.

Randi turned out to be far better than he had even thought she was going to be. And the woman only kept getting better and better with each passing month. To Sanford's relief and delight, he found that Randi actually did seem to love the boys. She went more than the extra mile when it came to them. She devoted herself to the boys, and it was obvious that they loved her for it. Sanford really didn't know what he would have done if he hadn't had her there, picking up his slack, looking over their homework as they got older and doing the hundred and one things that growing boys needed to be done.

Between missing Shirley and working long hours to keep his construction company going and earn a comfortable living for his five boys, Sanford was hardly around. There were times when Randi had to keep her employer in line, subtly of course, in order to avoid any hard feelings between Sanford and his sons.

It wasn't easy, but the kindhearted woman found a way to manage it all. She had always been extremely tactful, and she really did genuinely love her young charges through all the stages of their childhood, up to and including young manhood. Randi made certain that all five of the Sterling brothers were raised with a loving eye monitoring their progress.

Because of the circumstances that they were raised in, Randi made sure that she was always there for the young brothers. She tended to think of all the Sterling men as part of her own extended family, even Sanford, although she would never say anything to the man to make him think that she cared about him—although, in actuality, Randi really did.

So when she heard Sam on the other end of the phone line, Randi was nothing if not extremely surprised.

"Is anything wrong?" she asked, immediately trying to imagine what it might be.

All five of the Sterlings were grown young men now and always very busy with their careers. The last time she had heard from any of them was a few months ago. She knew for a fact that Sunday dinners were still very much a part of their lives, but she never assumed she was invited to attend unless an invitation was actually extended.

"No, nothing's wrong, Randi. I just thought I'd invite you to Sunday dinner this week," Sam told her.

To say she was surprised was putting it mildly. "That's very sweet of you, Sam," Randi told him. "Is there any particular reason why you're inviting me?"

"Maybe I just miss seeing you," Sam answered evasively.

Randi read between the lines. "Uh-huh. Now tell me the real reason you're inviting me to Sunday dinner."

She heard her former charge sigh deeply on the other end. "Well, if you need a reason," Sam told her, as if throwing up his hands in surrender, "I have a new assistant at the clinic."

"You mean you have an assistant at the clinic. If this person was a 'new' assistant, that means you would have had a previous assistant, and we both know that you've never had one before," she said knowingly.

"You really are a stickler for precision, aren't you, Randi?" Sam asked with a laugh.

"That's the only way to be accurate," Randi maintained. "That way, people won't have to wonder if you're being truthful or not."

Sam chuckled. "Ah, same old Randi."

"Hey, watch that 'old' stuff, son," the woman chided.

"And while you're at it, stop dancing around the subject. Be honest with me. Why are you inviting me over for Sunday dinner to meet your assistant? What makes him so special?"

She really hoped her former young charge wasn't attempting to match her up with someone. There was only one person who had won her heart, and she wasn't about to say anything about that. That would be the fastest way to get herself permanently banished from Sanford's table, and that was something she had no desire to do.

"Well, for one thing, he's a she," Sam told Randi, almost laughing.

Randi suppressed a cry of glee. "You're kidding," she exclaimed.

"No, I'm not," Sam told her. "She's a very nice person, and she wants to meet the woman who helped raise my brothers and me."

This was just getting better and better, Randi thought. "You told her about me?"

"The subject came up of who helped raise me after my mother died," Sam told her. "I wanted Gina to appreciate what a really wonderful person you are."

"Gina," Randi repeated. "Is she as pretty as her name?"

There was no point playing coy, Sam thought. If she came to Sunday dinner, Randi would be able to judge Gina's appearance for herself. "She is. So, will you come?"

Randi laughed under her breath. "You would have to tie me up and toss me into a closet to keep me from coming, boy," she said.

Sam laughed softly at the idea. "Nope, not planning on doing that."

"Good. Because being with you boys taught me a few things about how to get out of tight spots," Randi informed the young man she'd had the pleasure of watching grow into a vibrant adult.

"All right, I consider myself forewarned. So, should I tell Dad that you're going to be there this Sunday?" Sam asked.

"Absolutely," she told him with enthusiasm. "Shall I bring dessert?"

"No need," Sam told her. "Just having you there fulfills the requirement for something sweet."

Randi chuckled. "This Gina has certainly managed to change you."

"How so?" he asked.

"I don't remember you talking like that the last time we all got together. Is dinner the same time as always?" she asked, just in case things had changed.

"Same time," Sam assured her.

"I'll be there with bells on," she promised him.

"I'll let the others know that you're coming," Sam told her. "They'll all be happy to hear you'll be there for Sunday dinner. We've all missed you, Randi."

"And I've missed you. All of you," Randi said with emphasis. "See you Sunday."

* * *

Sam lost no time calling his father to let him know that Randi would be coming to dinner, along with Gina. He had planned to leave a message but was surprised to hear the line being picked up.

"Guess who's coming to dinner this Sunday, Dad," Sam said, getting over his surprise. His father hardly *ever* answered the phone.

"Tell me or don't tell me. I really don't have any time for games today, Sam," Sanford said, stopping short of being curt.

Sam took that to be his cue. "Randi is coming."

Like Randi, Sanford must have thought that her coming by had to mean that there was something wrong. "Anything wrong, Sam?"

"No, nothing's wrong. We just haven't seen her at the dinner table for a while. So I asked her to come by." Sam paused, then added, "Gina said she wanted to meet her, and I thought Sunday dinner would be the best setting."

"Gina *asked* to meet Randi?" Sanford asked, surprised.

"It was her idea," Sam told him. And then, just in case his father had some objection, he asked, "It is okay, isn't it?"

Sanford was glad there was no way Sam could see him; he was grinning so hard over the news, Sam would have known something was up. "Absolutely," Sanford assured his son. "I'd be curious to hear what

Gina has to say about the woman who devoted so much of her life to bringing you boys up right."

He heard Sam laughing to himself. "You, too, huh, Dad?"

"Well, this is the first young woman you've ever invited to the house for Sunday dinner—or anything else," his father pointed out. "That does make a difference, Sam."

"Don't make a big deal out of it, Dad," Sam told him uncomfortably.

"Not me," Sanford said innocently, as he hung up. "I'm not making a big deal out of anything."

And now, Sanford thought, the young woman had expressed an interest in meeting the nanny who'd helped raise all five of his sons. That spoke volumes. Gina was apparently becoming more entrenched in their day-to-day lives. This was a very good thing, and he intended to encourage that as subtly as he could, Sanford promised himself.

He glanced heavenward. "I really do miss you, Shirley. I think you would wholeheartedly approve of Gina," he said softly, his eyes misting over. "These last few years have really been a lonely struggle without you. Thank you for sending Randi my way to help out with the boys. I know that was your doing. There could be no other explanation for it. I know you've been right here beside me, guiding my every step when it comes to the boys, and I really do appreciate that," he whispered.

"Who are you talking to, Dad?" Sean asked, coming into the trailer that served as a mobile office on their current job site.

Sanford gave his youngest son a look meant to silence him.

Sean nodded as if the answer to his question suddenly occurred to him. "Oh."

"What do you mean, 'oh'?" Sanford asked, becoming defensive.

Sean smiled at him. "I realized you were talking to Mom."

"What would you know about it?" Sanford asked.

"You have a habit of talking to Mom when you have something on your mind," Sean said, and then he smiled. "I do pay attention, Dad."

"All right. Now try paying attention to the job," Sanford said, pointing toward the door.

"I do, Dad. Trust me, I do. I wouldn't want to incur your wrath by dropping the ball."

Sanford looked at him, perplexed. "Incur my wrath? Where do you get this stuff?"

Sean merely smiled. "I already told you, Dad. I pay attention to what's going on."

Sanford shook his head and murmured a few choice words under his breath as he went to walk around the worksite.

Chapter Twenty-Two

Sam noticed that Gina was acting somewhat nervous as they drove to his father's house the following Sunday afternoon. At first, he thought maybe he was imagining it. After all, she had taken on the position of being his assistant at the clinic without any difficulty whatsoever. Doing new things just seemed to come naturally for her. And she was the one who had asked him to arrange for her to meet Randi. Why, then, did she suddenly seem so nervous about this meeting? Had he missed something?

Rather than wait for Gina to say anything, he decided to come right out and ask her. "This might just be my imagination, but are you all right?"

She looked at him like she had her hand caught in a cookie jar. "Why do you ask?"

"You seem to be acting rather nervous," he told her.

Gina let out a long breath. She was being ridiculous, and she knew it, but she just couldn't help it. She really wanted this to go well. "Do you have any advice about what to say or not say when I meet your former nanny?" she asked him.

Coming to a stoplight, Sam glanced in Gina's direction. The question she asked didn't sound like her. "Are you nervous about meeting Randi?" he asked in disbelief.

"No," Gina denied a little too quickly. Then, in the next breath, she amended, "Yes," only to arrive at her ultimate reply, "Maybe."

That didn't make any sense to Sam. He was accustomed to Gina being bold and just forging ahead. Why was she waffling this way? This just wasn't like her. His assistant was an extremely strong person.

"For heaven's sake, why?" Sam asked. "You were the one who asked to meet her."

"I know, I know." Embarrassed, Gina shrugged. "You told me that Randi was and still is a very important person in your life. I just thought I should meet the woman who played such an instrumental part in raising you and your brothers."

"Well, she did," he agreed. "But that doesn't seem to be a reason for you to be so nervous about meeting her."

Before Gina could think twice about it, the answer came out: "Because I really want her to like me."

He glanced at Gina, not quite believing what he was hearing. Was this confident young woman afraid that his former nanny wouldn't like her? Why? "Don't worry," Sam assured the woman whom he had up until now thought of as the personification of confidence. "I guarantee that Randi will like you."

"You don't know that," Gina contended.

"Of course I do," Sam countered with feeling. "I know Randi. She is a sweet, loving woman who has great intuition about things that matter. That's why Dad picked her to be the one who helped raise us." He grew quiet for a moment. Then Sam confided, "I suspect that Randi reminded him a lot of my mother."

Gina was still concerned about the way this first meeting between her and Randi would go. "But what if she *doesn't* like me?"

Sam sincerely doubted there was any danger of that, but saying that most likely wouldn't reassure the woman he found himself falling in love with. So he went with the most logical response to her concerns.

"I could see how that might bother you, but in the grand scheme of things, that really doesn't matter," he said firmly. "Look, my father likes you, my brothers like you, and what matters most of all here, *I* like you. Is that good enough for you?" he asked, looking in her direction again.

Gina couldn't believe they had gotten so serious so quickly, but they had. This wasn't just some hypothetical conversation they were having, she thought. It seemed to her like it was a dead serious one. Some things, of course, were still left unspoken, but she had a feeling they would come to the surface eventually. At least, she could cross her fingers and sincerely hope so.

She gave Sam a fleeting smile. "Of course."

Sam slanted a quick look at her. "I'm not sure I believe you. But for now, I'll pretend that I do."

"Well, I'll take whatever I can get," she answered. "And as for why this is important to me, I always do better if I feel like I'm in a friendly situation where I'm not the object of angry looks."

Sam pulled his vehicle alongside one of his brothers' cars. It looked to him as if everyone was already there. He needed to learn how to arrive earlier, he thought, instead of being the last one in the door.

"Looks like we get to make a grand entrance," he told Gina, turning off the engine.

Now that they were finally here, she could feel her nerves going into double time. Gina frowned slightly, looking at the other vehicles in front of the two-storied house. "Not exactly what I was hoping for," she admitted.

"Well," he told her, "we can turn around and go back to the clinic." Sam looked at her face, trying to gauge what she was thinking.

Gina stared at him as if he had just lost his mind. "No, we can't," she protested. As nervous as she was, she wanted to meet this woman. It was a hurdle that would only grow higher the more she put it off.

"Sure we can," he countered. "We can do anything we want to."

Gina looked at him as if he was just paying lip service to an uncomfortable situation. "No, we can't," she repeated. "I asked you to invite your nanny to Sunday dinner so I could finally get to meet her."

But he was ready to slip out if that made her feel better. He just wanted her to know that he was in her corner. "I won't say anything if you don't," Sam told her.

Her brow furrowed. "You're serious," she said in surprise.

Sam's eyes lightly washed over her. She felt as if they were caressing her. He drew closer to her until they were only inches apart. "Very," he whispered.

The word seemed to ripple along her skin, warming her to the point that she felt she needed to fan herself. "I'll accept that," she told him, attempting to regulate her pulse.

"Sure you want to go in?" Sam asked.

He was not making this easy for her, she thought. "I am utterly sure that I want to go in," Gina answered, squaring her shoulders.

Sam presented his arm to her. "Then let's do this."

"Happily," she answered. Her heart slammed against her rib cage as Sam opened the front door and ushered her in front of him.

"So what is she like?" Randi was asking Sanford. "Is she a nice person?"

Instead of answering himself, he looked toward his sons. "You guys want to take that one?" he asked.

As the youngest, Sean felt it was up to him to answer. "You are going to really love her, Randi. She actually talked Sam into making her his assistant at the clinic, and you know how long he held off doing that. She puts in long hours helping him take care of the animals, and when there are no patients, she's busy digitizing all the files."

Meanwhile, Sam was leaning his head in toward Gina so she could hear what he was telling her as they came into the house. "Breathe, Gina, breathe," he whispered to her. Her face was slightly flushed. Up until now, he'd had no idea that meeting Randi meant so much to her. He felt touched and concerned at the same time.

"I am breathing," Gina protested as she watched six pairs of eyes turn in her direction.

His father and brothers were, as usual, all here ahead of Sam. And there was one rather attractive-looking woman seated at the center of the table, smiling at them as they entered. This had to be Randi, the woman who'd helped raise all five of the Sterling brothers. Gina held her breath as her eyes met the woman's.

At that moment, Randi got up and came toward her, hands held out to the first young woman who had ever come to their table. The man she had spent these last twenty years working for had told her all about how his oldest son had taken to this young woman. According to Sanford, Gina had made an "unexpected" appearance at the clinic in the middle of the night with her injured dog, and Sam, being the dedicated veterinarian that he was, had immediately brought the miniature collie into his clinic and sewn up her wounds. In apparent gratitude, the young woman had volunteered her services and offered to work for Sam, organizing his files or whatever else needed doing to get the clinic running smoothly.

Randi found herself liking the young woman immediately. Her eyes crinkled as she took Gina's hands in hers. "Hello. I've heard very good things about you," she said.

"And I you," Gina responded, relieved at the display of friendship. "Sam told me all about how you helped raise him and his brothers. And how much you helped him study for his exams when he decided to become a veterinarian."

Genuine warmth emanated from the former nanny, creating an exceedingly good feeling within Gina. The brothers might have been deprived of their mother during their formative years, and that was an awful thing, but it seemed to Gina that this woman had done whatever she could to help make up for the tragic loss. The fact that all five brothers had gone on to college and done well in their chosen fields was a testament to how much Randi had cared for them, even when they had all gone on to earn different degrees in different fields.

Randi waved her hand, dismissing the praise. "Sam was a self-starter. Actually, all the boys were," she told Gina. "I did what I could to help set them on the right path, but they did most of the work." She smiled, remembering those years. "It was quite an education for me as well." She looked around the table, getting down to business. "Who made dinner today?"

Scott raised his hand. "That would be me, Randi. But I didn't do the dessert."

Randi looked as if she was about to head over to the kitchen counter immediately. "I can whip up a batch of chocolate chip cookies, provided I can find all the ingredients." She had enjoyed baking for years.

"No need, Randi," Sam told her. "Gina wanted to make a batch of her killer cookies to show you her gratitude for coming to Sunday dinner so she could meet you."

"Her gratitude?" Randi echoed in disbelief. "I have been waiting for an invitation to meet this young woman. If I hadn't received one soon, I would have forgotten about being polite and happily crashed this little Sunday tradition of yours." She looked at the faces around the table, her face softening. "I have really missed you boys—and now I will have someone new to miss the next time you all forget to invite me on a regular basis."

Gina flashed a smile at the older woman. "I'll be sure to remind them," she told Randi.

Sam smiled to himself. The two most important women in his life were bonding—and he, for one, was absolutely thrilled about it.

Chapter Twenty-Three

"I like her," Randi told Sam.

Sam nodded, pleased to hear his former nanny's assessment of the woman who had effortlessly captured his heart. Dinner was over, and Randi and Sam were cleaning up the kitchen at Randi's insistence because she wanted to have a word with him. "I'll be sure to tell her, Randi. I know that Gina will be very pleased," he assured the woman he regarded so highly.

"Never mind me, Sam," Randi told him. "Whether or not I like her is beside the point. That girl needs to hear those words coming from you—that *you* like her," she emphasized.

"Oh, I think she already knows that," he said casually.

"Because you told her?" Randi asked, watching Sam's face to get some sort of confirmation on the matter.

"I don't have to," Sam insisted. "Gina's pretty good like that. She just intuits things."

Randi sighed as she rolled her eyes. "Oh, Samuel, Samuel, Samuel, I raised you better than that. Some things you just cannot take for granted, no matter how much easier it is to go that route. Women need to *hear* those comforting words, boy. As do men," Randi added pointedly. "This is not just a one-way street. You're a smart guy. I would have expected you to know that."

Sam shrugged as he continued to wash dishes. "I've been a little busy running the clinic."

"Which, according to my sources, Gina has been helping you with," Randi said.

His mouth curved. "It looks like you're more caught up with my life than I am," Sam said.

"I make a point of keeping up on the lives of the people I care about," Randi told him.

"Who's your source?" he asked her point-blank.

Randi laughed as she set aside the last dish she had dried. "Oh, no, that stays with me, Samuel," she said. "Am I right? You haven't told that young woman how you feel? I can see it, right there in your eyes."

"Well, if it's right there in my eyes, then I don't have to say anything, do I?" he asked, amused.

"You know better than that," Randi told him. "Those particular words are always nice to hear. C'mon, boy," she urged. "I never thought of you as being a coward."

The accusation took him aback. "I am not a coward," he protested.

"Then what's stopping you from telling that girl what you just admitted to me?" she asked.

"What if she doesn't feel the same way?" he asked.

He would have hated to bare his soul and then just be pushed away.

"Oh, come on, boy," Randi said, waving away his fears. "That young woman definitely feels the same way about you as you do about her."

Gina chose that moment to come into the kitchen and quickly looked from Sam to Randi. "Are you two still washing dishes?" she asked, surprised. "Even if you were doing them in slow motion, you should have been finished by now."

Randi chuckled. "Like I said, Samuel, this young woman is very likable." As she made her way around her former charge, she whispered in his ear, "It took you long enough, but when you finally got around to picking someone, you certainly made the right choice." She patted his arm in approval.

Turning toward Gina, Randi said, "It's been a pleasure, dear, and one I hope will be repeated. Very happy to meet you."

Gina waited until the woman left the room and then looked toward Sam. "What was that all about?"

"That was Randi giving you her seal of approval," Sam explained.

"She's too sweet to do anything short of that," Gina commented. "Your dad picked a really nice woman to take care of you guys."

"There is no arguing with that," he agreed. He hung up the towel Randi had been using. "Well, the kitchen's all cleaned up. What do you think of us hitting the road and going back home?" he asked. "I'd say that right about now, Rocky and Charlotte are really beginning to miss us."

Gina nodded. "You're probably right. Heaven knows that I certainly miss them. I can be ready to leave in a few minutes. Just let me make the rounds and say my goodbyes."

"I really appreciate that," he said suddenly. "As do my brothers and my dad," Sam threw in, just in case the woman who had won his heart hadn't realized that.

The smile she gave him was positively blinding.

"Someone famous once said *always leave them wanting more*," Gina told him brightly. "So this might be a good time to go."

Randi was just about to go home herself, but she paused long enough to give Gina a warm, heartfelt hug in parting. "Lovely finally meeting you, my dear. I hope this is the beginning of a long, wonderful tradition," Randi told her with enthusiasm. Releasing her, Randi added, "Soon," making it sound like a promise.

Gina glanced toward Sam's father. "I certainly hope so," she replied, looking from Sanford back to Randi. Her meaning was extremely clear.

For a moment, Randi remained standing beside the man she had worked for all these long years. She eyed Sanford. "That is one very lovely young girl," she told him with feeling.

"Careful, Randi," Sanford warned. "Your age is

showing. Sam's new assistant isn't a girl. She's a young woman."

Randi laughed softly to herself. "Since when did you get to be such an expert on proper terms?"

"I pay attention," Sanford told her with a touch of indignation.

Randi's smile only grew wider. "If you say so, Mr. Sterling."

"Why? Don't you think I pay attention?" he asked her.

Randi feigned surprise, placing her hand on her chest. "Me? Of course I think you pay attention. I never said anything to the contrary, Mr. Sterling." It was hard to keep her smile from completely taking over.

Sanford gave her a knowing look. "Uh-huh. You would be more convincing if you weren't grinning so hard, Randi."

Randi winked at the man she still thought of in fond terms. "I'll work on it, Mr. Sterling."

"You know, I think it might be high time for you to refer to me as Sanford, or at least stop referring to me as Mr. Sterling," Sanford told her.

"I'd be happy to comply." She glanced toward the front door.

Without a family of her own, and after all the years she spent raising them, Randi had a real tendency to think of the Sterling boys as her own sons. In truth, the five young men represented the family she had never been blessed with in real life. Her eyes swept lovingly over the ones who hadn't left yet for their own homes this evening: Sean, Scott and, of course, Sam.

She placed her hand on Sam's shoulder the way she used to when he was a little boy. It had been her way of holding him to something he had said.

"Until next week, then?" she asked him, searching his face for confirmation.

Sam smiled and nodded. "Until next week, Randi." He made the words sound more like a promise than just a throwaway remark.

Gina leaned in and echoed, "Until next week."

She could take it for granted that she herself would be invited back to sit at the large family dinner table. It felt nice, she thought, to feel as if she belonged to something after all these years of *not* belonging to anything. This had been a long time in coming, but she had finally achieved that dream, and her insides felt as if they were doing cartwheels and cheering all the way.

Inspired, Gina squeezed both Randi's and Sanford's hands and then leaned in to brush a kiss on each of their cheeks.

The only time she had ever felt happier was after she made love with Sam. But this, Gina thought, was an extremely close second.

Chapter Twenty-Four

They had put in another grueling day at the clinic. This was on top of several days just like it when they worked practically from dawn to dusk. Of course, that was broken up with making love, sometimes late in the evening, sometimes in the wee hours of the morning. Looking forward to those moments was what kept them going.

They took turns staying at each other's homes, although for the most part, they stayed at Sam's because of its proximity to the clinic. That and the fact that they both wanted to be near the animals kept at the clinic overnight.

Through it all, neither Sam nor Gina could remember ever being happier.

"So, things seem to be going pretty well between you and Gina," Simon noted one Sunday, taking his older brother aside after dinner.

Sam had been clearing up dinner with Gina, but she had temporarily stepped away from the kitchen. Simon had seen it as his opportunity to talk to Sam alone.

Sam braced himself, thinking that he was about to get a lecture from the divorce lawyer about getting into something that could have dire consequences. He tried to keep his response civil. "No offense, Simon, but I'm just not in the mood for a lawyer lecture right now."

Simon's eyebrows drew together in a dark line over the bridge of his nose. "Who said anything about giving you a lecture?"

"Isn't that why you waited until I was alone to talk to me?" Sam asked.

"You have a very suspicious mind, big brother." Simon laughed shortly. "I might have said that I'm soured on the subject of marriage, but I wasn't looking to set an example for the rest of you—especially when you seem to have found the only woman who has a heart of gold and shares your love of animals."

Sam looked at his brother, curious. "What makes you think Gina has a heart of gold?"

Simon laughed, waving his hand at Sam. "Hey, I have eyes. I get paid for having sound judgment and observing things."

Where was this leading? Sam wondered. "And?"

"And Gina seems like a terrific person who came into your life even though the rest of us could definitely have used that sunshine that she's spreading."

"And I can't?" Sam questioned.

"I never said that," Simon pointed out. "I just wanted you to know exactly what you have here." Then, in case there was any question on Sam's part, Simon made his position crystal clear. "Gina is a very rare, special young woman, and if you don't get your act together and ask her to marry you, I predict that you're running the very real risk of losing her."

Sam's attention was riveted on Simon now. "Why? What have you heard?"

"Nothing specific. I just have great intuition," Simon casually declared.

Sam couldn't believe what he was hearing, especially not from Simon. "So you're advising me to propose to her?"

Simon didn't answer immediately. Instead, he asked, "Do you love her?"

Sam thought on the matter before finally saying, "Yes."

"Then what the hell are you waiting for?" Simon asked.

Sam shook his head in wonder. "You know, I never thought I'd be hearing this coming from you."

"Yeah, well, I never thought I'd be the one saying it, either." Simon's lips pulled back in a smile. "But I am. I think that our brothers are all half in love with her as well, so if I were you, I'd snap her up before one of the others decides to sweep her off her feet while you're dawdling around."

Out of the corner of his eye, Sam saw movement near the doorway. He instinctively knew it was Gina, so he was smiling broadly by the time he turned toward her. "Have you been there long?"

"Long enough," she answered, her eyes smiling at Sam.

Simon pulled back his shoulders. "I guess this is my cue to leave," the lawyer announced. He paused for a moment. "If you find that you ever want to move on from this guy, I've got files that need to be reorganized. You know where to find me," he told Gina, then left the kitchen.

"I guess you made a really good impression on my brothers," Sam said, replaying in his head what Simon had told him. "But then, I would have expected nothing less—from you and from them."

Gina looked at him uncertainly. "Are you trying to get rid of me?"

How had she managed to get that out of what he'd just said? "Are you serious?" he asked in disbelief.

"Well..." Her voice trailed off as she shrugged.

"There's no way I'm trying to get rid of you," he assured her. "As a matter of fact, I'm trying to find a way to ask you the most important question of my life."

And possibly of my life as well, Gina thought. Out loud, she told him, "I'm listening."

He took a deep breath, feeling like the air had gotten stuck in his throat. He had never had trouble verbalizing his thoughts before, but right now, they were all jumbled in his head.

She couldn't put up with watching him suffer through

this—which was why, before Sam could put words to his thoughts, she told him, "Yes."

"Yes?" he asked, slightly confused. Was she saying what he thought she was, or was that just wishful thinking on his part?

Gina smiled widely and repeated her answer. "Yes."

Afraid of getting carried away, he wanted to be sure that they were both clear about this. "Just what are you saying yes to?" he asked.

"I am saying yes to the phrase that is apparently stuck in your throat," Gina said. And then she took a deep breath, plunging in feetfirst, praying she hadn't just made a really huge mistake. "You are asking me to marry you, right?"

The look of total relief on Sam's face was impossible to miss. "Yes," he told her, "I am asking you to marry me."

"Then for heaven's sake, do it," Gina urged him. "Say the words." Then, if there was any confusion as to what she was telling him, she said, "Ask me to marry you."

Every woman deserved to hear those words, he thought, if that was what she wanted. So, taking a deep breath, Sam plunged in.

"Gina, will you make me the happiest man on the face of the earth and say yes? Say that you will marry me?" he asked his assistant, making it official. And then he added, "Bearing in mind that if you turn me down, you will not just be breaking my heart, but the hearts of all my brothers as well as my father's and the woman who raised me."

Gina laughed, shaking her head. "No pressure there."

"Nope," he agreed. "None." His eyes crinkled as he looked at her, impatient to hear the words. "Well?"

Gina look in a long breath, her eyes meeting his.

"Hey," Sean called out, coming into the kitchen. "You guys washing the dishes or forging new ones?" He looked from Sam to Gina, his eyebrows raised quizzically.

Sam frowned at him. "You know, your timing couldn't have been worse."

It took Sean a couple of moments to untangle that. Then suddenly light dawned on his face. "Oh, I'm sorry. I can leave." He turned on his heel, ready to make his way out of the room again.

"No need," Gina quickly assured him. "We're almost finished cleaning up here."

Sean looked a little uncertain, glancing from his brother to the first woman besides their nanny to be invited to Sunday dinner. "Is that all I interrupted?" he asked suspiciously.

Sam slanted a look at Gina. Maybe she wanted to take this time as a reprieve. Maybe she really didn't want him asking her to marry him. He had been so focused on making her his wife that he hadn't thought the idea might not appeal to her to the same degree it did him.

Things felt as if they were stuck in a holding pattern, and he desperately wanted to get them moving again. "Gina, could I talk to you?" he asked her.

She glanced toward Sean. "You don't want to be rude to your brother."

Sam laughed. "Sean has a skin that's tough as a rhino's," he told her. "He wouldn't know rude if he tripped over it."

"See what I have to put up with?" Sean asked Gina. "I'd be very careful if I were you. You're hooking your star to a man who is as kindly as a splinter."

Sam's eyebrows drew together. "She doesn't need to hear that from you."

"Well, she needs to hear it from someone," Sean pointed out.

Both brothers turned almost in unison toward Gina, who laughed.

"Something funny?" Sam asked.

"You guys are. I never had a close family," she said for the umpteenth time. "And I am really enjoying the way you all play off one another."

Sam breathed a sigh of relief. He had allowed his fears to temporarily paralyze him and keep him from moving on. Maybe because he wanted her so badly that he was fearful of losing her.

Sam made up his mind right then and there.

He needed to subtly feel her out in order to make sure that Gina was up to this, that all her talk about sharing things with a family was something she truly wanted. Once he was sure of that, then he would proceed with a proposal next Sunday in front of everyone. If anything would make her feel part of the family, it would be that.

The moment he made his decision, he knew it was the way to go.

Chapter Twenty-Five

Sam had never felt this nervous before. Not even when he took his exam to get certified for his veterinarian license. He had been very confident about that, he recalled. But the stakes were higher now, and he wasn't confident any longer. He felt a little like a trapeze artist about to take a flying leap without a net beneath him.

Sam had a feeling that Gina wouldn't exactly take kindly to the description, but butterflies were practically dive-bombing all throughout his stomach. He could honestly say his stomach felt tied up in proverbial knots.

Hell, this wasn't like him. He had treated animals that could by no stretch of the imagination be called friendly.

What if she turned him down? Wouldn't this be easier for him to do if he were more confident of her mindset? He rubbed his damp hands against his jeans to no avail.

It would have been wiser if he did this in private, without an audience.

Wiser, maybe, but definitely more cowardly. Since this was the first proposal to happen within their family since his parents, he knew it had to be special. He had to put his best foot forward. And that involved asking Gina to marry him in front of everyone at the Sunday dinner table.

Of course, he was hoping that she would say yes. Hoping, but since he was a realist, he wasn't counting on it—at least, not 100 percent. He vacillated over that outcome. When she was in his arms, and they were in bed, he felt confident that she would say yes. But once they were in the clinic, going about the life that they were so dedicated to, his confidence was not quite as strong about the answer that awaited him.

He just needed to ask, to pop the question and roll with the answer. All he could do was pray she would take pity on him and say yes.

Why wouldn't she say yes? Their relationship wasn't all in his head, he silently argued with himself as they drove to his father's house the following Sunday. He didn't have that good of an imagination.

Gina turned toward him. A question had been nagging at her for the last week, and she finally decided to put it into words. "Are you all right?" she asked Sam.

"Yes," he answered. His curiosity got the better of him. "Why do you ask?"

Sam was the first man she had given her heart to.

Her heart as well as her body, she thought ruefully, and she had no idea what to expect. Was he growing leery or withdrawing from her? Maybe this was what the end looked like, she thought, and she was just too naive to realize it. Their working relationship would be an added complication. Maybe Sam didn't want to say anything because he was afraid she would quit the clinic. Never mind that this was her ideal job. What she was experiencing with Sam just raised that to new heights.

She felt as if she had just built a house of cards and a windstorm was on its way.

She realized that Sam was waiting for her to tell him why she had asked if there was anything wrong.

"Well, for the last few days, you've been tossing and turning in bed instead of sleeping," she pointed out. "That usually happens when a person has something on their mind." She pressed her lips together. "I'm not trying to pry. But if there's something wrong, I just want to help."

You can, he thought. *You can say yes.* But Sam knew that was a dangerous way to go if he didn't immediately elaborate. Instead, he told her, "I appreciate that," and hoped that would satisfy her for the time being.

But it didn't.

"I didn't say that so you would appreciate it. I meant what I said. I want to help you," she insisted.

"In order to do that, you have to tell me what's bothering you."

Sitting up straight in the driver's seat and keeping his face forward, Sam kept his expression from registering anything, afraid she could read something in it. He shrugged and went with the ever-popular "It's complicated."

"I assumed that. If it wasn't complicated, you would have said something about it already," she told him. "Either that, or you would have just handled it yourself."

He sighed. Part of him wanted to blurt out the proposal right here and now. But he had already run this by his father, and his family was expecting him to propose to Gina in front of all of them. He definitely didn't want to disappoint them or come off like a coward in front of all his younger brothers.

Sam blew out a breath. "It's nothing for you to worry about."

Gina felt an overwhelming sadness wash over her. He was blocking her out. And here she had believed that they were a team. *Looks like I was wrong*, Gina thought. Maybe she wasn't as integral a part of his team as she had thought.

"All right," she declared gamely, going along with him. "If you don't want to share, you don't want to share. Either way, we need to get ready to open up the clinic. Your first patient is coming in at seven."

Well, that hadn't gone well, Sam thought. He couldn't wait until this was completely behind him—provided he heard the answer he was hoping to hear. Watching this play out in front of him in slow motion was all but killing him.

When Sam and Gina walked into the Sterling house several hours later, Sanford immediately gravitated to his oldest son. One look at Sam's face told him that the secret was still a secret.

"You look like you've seen a ghost, son," Sanford commented.

"Yeah, I've seen more color in a bottle of milk," Sean told his brother. "You feeling okay?"

"That's what I asked him," Gina told them.

"I take it he wasn't exactly forthcoming," Simon guessed.

"The dogs at the clinic are more talkative," Gina said. "We checked on them just before we came here."

Randi chuckled as she came in from the kitchen, drying her hands. "So he has you talking to the animals, too. Knew it would just be a matter of time before he indoctrinated you. In my opinion, you two are very suited for one another."

Then she seemed to notice the way Sam and his father looked at her. "What? Am I wrong?" she asked.

Sanford shook his head. "No, just sometimes, Randi, you talk a little too much."

Randi laughed, shaking her head. "That's to make

up for the fact that you guys don't talk at all. Think of me as a counterbalance to all your tight-lipped behavior."

Gina turned toward Sam, her eyebrows drawing together. "Why are they talking in code like that?" she asked.

He had his doubts that anyone was fooling Gina. She was exceptionally bright and able to catch on to any situation rather quickly. Still, he felt it was time to be completely honest with her. "Because they've never been part of a real live proposal before."

Gina looked at Sam, her heart slamming against her chest. Telling herself to be calm and not jump to any conclusions, she said, "Oh? Then I suggest you get on with it."

Sam squared his shoulders, ready to plunge right into this. Apparently, Gina knew more about what was going on than he gave her credit for. It figured. He had spent more time worrying about the way this would come off than he had actually spent wording the proposal.

His hand felt clammy as he reached into his pocket. The ring box was beginning to feel rather heavy, and for a moment, he had some difficulty pulling the small black velvet box out of the recesses of his pants. Pulling hard, he managed to extract it from where it was wedged.

Sam felt as if his insides were actually trembling. At the last moment, he remembered the form he needed to hit and dropped down to one knee. He pushed open the small box, and the diamond ring caught the light, sending a rainbow twinkling and dancing around for the entire audience looking on.

All around him, his brothers were smiling and poking one another. Sam drew in a long breath, then began to tell her what was in his heart.

"Gina, my whole world changed when you came into it. And now I can't imagine life without you there or without you in the clinic," he confessed. What he was saying might not be as romantic as it could have been, but he was telling her what he felt. "Will you make me the happiest of men and say that you'll be my wife?"

Gina stared at him. Everything felt incredibly numb inside of her. "You're serious?" she finally asked, her mouth so dry that her lips were all but sticking together.

"I've never been more serious in my life," Sam told the woman he had first met banging on his door in the middle of the night.

"Oh, come on. Put the poor guy out of his misery already," Sebastian urged.

"Hey, I don't believe in the sacred institution, and even I'm thinking that you were made for one another," Simon told the couple, smiling from Sam to Gina.

Gina dropped to her knees right in front of Sam, putting out her hand so that he could slip the ring onto the proper finger. Trying to keep from trembling, she held her breath, waiting.

Sanford couldn't begin to say how happy he was watching this unfold in front of him. He had picked this woman as the right one for his son, and he was glorying in what he had set in motion. But he kept his enthusiasm to himself, waiting for Sam to make it official.

"Give him an answer, dear," Randi prompted Gina. "Put the sweet boy out of his misery."

"What if her answer just pushes him further into his misery?" Sebastian asked.

Gina waved her hand at the men about to become her brothers-in-law. "No offense, guys, but I don't need a Greek chorus behind either one of us telling us what to say."

"That's right, dear. This is all up to you," Randi said. "Give him his answer, because I am dying to hug you."

Gina's smile all but took over her entire face. "Gladly." Still on her knees, she looked at the man who had brought such changes into her life. "Yes, Sam."

"Yes, what?" Sam asked, wanting it all to be perfectly clear, not just to her, but to the rest of his family as well.

"Yes, I will marry you," Gina told him.

The rest of her words were drowned out by the cheers of congratulations that erupted in the room.

Dinner, at least for the time being, was all but forgotten.

Sanford went and retrieved the bottle of champagne he had been saving in anticipation just for this day.

One down, Sanford thought, *four to go.*

* * * * *

SPECIAL EXCERPT FROM

When ex-con Wes Calhoun moves into Bramble-berry House, his neighbor Jenna Haynes gives him a wide berth. Widowed and the former target of a stalker, the single mom errs on the side of extreme caution when it comes to men—and her heart. Jenna vows to keep a neighborly distance. Until she needs help—but should she trust an ex-con with her heart or safely lock it up and throw away the key?

Read on for a sneak preview of
A Beach House Beginning
by RaeAnne Thayne.

Chapter One

"Jenna? Are you still there?"

Jenna Haynes slowly lowered herself to one of the kitchen chairs of her apartment on the second floor of Brambleberry House. Her cell phone nearly slipped from fingers that suddenly trembled.

"I… Yes. I'm here." Her voice sounded hollow, thready.

"I know this must be coming as a shock to you." Angela Terry, the prosecuting attorney who had worked on the Oregon part of her case, spoke in a low, calming voice. "Believe me, we were all stunned, too. I never expected this. I'm sorry to call you so early but I wanted to reach out to you as soon as we heard the news."

"Thank you. I appreciate that."

"Seriously, what a shock. It's so hard to believe, when Barker was only halfway through his sentence. Who expects a guy in the prime of his life to go to sleep in his cell one night and never wake up? You know what they say. Karma drives a big bus and she knows everybody's address."

Jenna didn't know how to answer, still trying to process the stunning news that the man she had feared for three years was truly gone.

On the heels of her shock came an overwhelming relief. A man was dead. She couldn't forget that. Still, the man had made her life a nightmare for a long time.

"You're…you're positive he's dead?"

"The warden called me to confirm it himself, as soon as the medical examiner determined it was from natural causes. An aneurysm."

"An aneurysm? Seriously?"

"That's what the warden said. Who knows, Barker might have had a brain anomaly all along. What else would cause a decorated police officer to go off the rails like he did and spend years stalking, threatening and finally attacking you and others?"

Jenna fought down an instinctive shiver as the terrifying events of two years earlier crawled out from the lockbox of memories where she tried to store them for safekeeping.

Dead. The boogeyman who had haunted her nightmares for so long was gone.

She still couldn't quite believe it, even hearing it from a woman she trusted and admired, a woman who had fought hard to make sure Aaron Barker would remain behind bars for the maximum allowable sentence, which had been entirely too short a time, as far as Jenna was concerned.

Jenna didn't know how she was supposed to feel, now that she knew he couldn't get out to pick up where he'd left off.

"I'm sorry to call so early. I hope I didn't wake you, but I wanted you to know as soon as possible."

The concern in her voice warmed Jenna. Angela had been an unending source of calm and comfort, even during the most stressful of times during the trial.

"No. I'm glad you called. I appreciate it."

Slowly, her brain seemed to reengage and she remembered the polite niceties she owed this woman who had fought with such fierce determination for her.

"You didn't wake me," she assured Angela. "I have school this morning."

"Oh, good. I was hoping I didn't catch you while you were sleeping in on your first day of summer vacation or something."

"One more week for that," Jenna answered. "I'm just fixing breakfast for Addie."

"How is my little buddy? Tell her we need to get together soon for a *Mario Kart* rematch. No way can I let a seven-year-old get the better of me."

"Eight. She turned eight last month."

"Already? Dang. I can't believe I missed her birthday. I'll have to send her something."

"You don't have to do that, Angela. You've done

so much already for us. I can never thank you enough for everything. I mean that."

"Well, we still need to get together and catch up. It's been too long."

"Yes. I would love that. I'll only be working part-time at the gift shop this summer, so my schedule is much more flexible than during the school year."

"We'll do it. We can have Rosa join us. I'll set up a text string and we can work out details."

"Thank you for telling me about Aaron."

"I know you had been worrying about his release next year," the other woman said, her voice gentle. "I hope that knowing he can't ever bother you again goes a little way toward taking a weight off your heart."

"It does. I can't even tell you how much."

They spoke for a few more moments before ending the call with promises to make plans later in the summer.

Jenna set her phone on the table slowly, released a heavy sigh and then covered her face with her hands.

Dead.

She didn't quite know how to react.

Since the arrest and conviction eighteen months ago of the man who had tormented her for years, she had been bracing herself for the moment when he might be released, when she might have to pick up her daughter again and flee.

She had hated the idea of it.

Brambleberry House, this beautiful rambling beach house on the dramatic coastline of northern Oregon, had become a haven for them. She had finally begun to rebuild her life here, to feel safe again and…happy.

Lurking at the edge of her consciousness, though, like the dark, far-off blur of an impending storm, was the grim realization that someday she might have to leave everything once more and start again somewhere else.

Now she didn't have to.

She wiped away tears she hadn't even realized were coursing down her cheeks.

He was gone. They were free.

"What's wrong, Mom?"

She turned to find her daughter in the doorway, wearing shorts, a ruffled T-shirt and a frown.

Jenna gave a laugh and reached for Addie, pulling her into a tight hug.

"Nothing's wrong. Everything is terrific. Really terrific."

Her perceptive child wasn't fooled. She eased away, narrowing her gaze. "What's going on?"

Jenna didn't want to talk about Aaron Barker. She didn't want Addie to have to think about the man who had threatened them both, who had completely upended their lives simply because he couldn't have what he wanted.

"Nothing." She gave a reassuring smile. "I'm just happy, that's all. It's a beautiful day, school will be out next week and summer is right around the corner. Now hurry and finish your breakfast so we can get to school. I could use your help carrying the cupcakes for my class."

Addie still didn't look convinced. Sometimes she seemed far too wise for her eight years on the earth. Apparently she decided not to push the matter.

"Can I have one of the cupcakes? You said I could when we were frosting them last night."

The cupcakes were a treat for her class, a reward for everyone meeting their reading goals for the year.

Jenna pointed to the counter, at a covered container near the microwave. "I've got two there for us. I was going to save them for dessert later tonight after dinner, but I suddenly feel like celebrating. Let's have a cupcake."

Addie's eyes widened with shock and then delight. She reached for the container and pulled out one of the chocolate cupcakes, biting into it quickly as if afraid Jenna would change her mind.

"You still have to eat your egg bites and your cantaloupe," Jenna warned.

"I don't care. Cupcakes for breakfast is the best idea ever."

She couldn't disagree, Jenna thought as she finished hers, as well as her own healthier breakfast. Still, the call was at the forefront of her thoughts as she hurried through the rest of her preparations for the school day.

Twenty minutes later, she juggled her laptop bag, a box of cupcakes and a stack of math papers she had graded the evening before.

She couldn't help humming a song as she walked out of her apartment, Addie right behind her.

A man stood on the landing outside her apartment, hand on the banister. He was big, dark, muscular, wearing a leather jacket and carrying a motorcycle helmet under his arm.

For one ridiculous moment, her heart skipped a beat, as it always did when she saw her new upstairs neighbor. Her song died and she immediately felt foolish.

"Morning," he said, voice gruff.

"Um. Hi."

"You've got your arms full. Can I help you carry something?"

"No. I've got it," she said, her voice more clipped than she intended.

His eyes darkened slightly at her abrupt tone. Something flickered in his expression, something hard and dangerous, but he merely nodded and gestured for them to go ahead of him down the stairs.

Did he guess she was afraid of him? Jenna had tried to hide it, but she strongly suspected she hadn't been very successful.

"Come on, Addie."

Her daughter, who seemed to have none of Jenna's

instinctive fear of big, tough, ruthless-looking men with more ink than charm, smiled and waved at him.

"Bye, Mr. Calhoun. I hope you have a happy day."

He looked nonplussed. "Thanks. Same to you."

Jenna led their little procession down the central staircase of Brambleberry House, which featured private entrances to the three apartments, one on each floor.

As she hurried outside, she couldn't help wondering again what Rosa Galvez Townsend had been thinking to rent the space to this man.

She had heard the rumors about Wes Calhoun. He had a daughter who attended her school, and while Brielle was a grade older and wasn't in Jenna's class, the girl's teacher was one of Jenna's closest friends.

Teachers gossiped as much as, if not more than, other populations. As soon as Wes Calhoun rode into town on his motorcycle, leather jacket, tattoos and all, Jenna had learned he was an ex-con only released a few months earlier from prison in the Chicago area.

Learning he would be her new upstairs neighbor had been unsettling and upsetting.

Rosa—who functioned as landlady for her aunt Anna and Anna's friend Sage, owners of the house—assured her he was a friend of Wyatt, Rosa's husband, and perfectly harmless. He had been wrongfully convicted three years earlier and had been completely cleared, his record expunged.

That didn't set her mind at ease. At all. She would have found the man intimidating even if she hadn't known he was only a few months out of prison.

She hurried Addie to her small SUV, loaded the cupcakes into the cargo area and made sure Addie was safely belted into the back.

As she slid behind the wheel, Jenna watched Wes climb onto his sleek, black death trap of a motorcycle parked beside her and fasten his helmet.

While he started up the bike, he didn't go anywhere, just waited, boots on the driveway. He was waiting for her, she realized.

Aware of his gaze on her, steely and unflinching, she tried the ignition.

Instead of purring to life, the car only gave an ominous click.

She tried it a second time, with the same results, then a third.

No. Oh, no. This wasn't happening. She was already running late.

Normally she and Addie could ride bikes the mile and a half to the school, but not when she had two dozen cupcakes to deliver!

Hoping against hope, she tried it a few more times, with the same futile click.

"What's wrong?" Addie asked.

"I'm not sure. The car isn't starting, for some reason."

A sudden knock at her window made her jump.

Without power, she couldn't lower the window, so she opened the door a crack.

"Having trouble?" Wes Calhoun looked at her with concern.

She wanted to tell him no, that she was a strong, independent woman who could handle her own problems. But what she knew about cars could probably fit inside one spark plug. If cars even had spark plugs anymore, which she suspected they didn't.

"You could say that. It won't start. I'm not getting anything but clicks."

"Sounds like it might be your battery. Do you know how old it is?"

"No. I bought the car used two years ago. It was three years old then. I have no idea how old the battery is. I do know I haven't replaced it."

"Pop the hood and I'll take a look at it."

"You don't have to do that. I can call road service."

He gave her a long look. "You seemed in a hurry this morning. Do you have time to wait for road service? If it's your battery, I can give you a jump and get you on the road in only a few minutes."

She glanced at her watch. The phone call with Angela had thrown off her whole morning schedule. She was already going to be late, without adding in a potentially long wait for road service.

"Thank you. I would appreciate a jump, if you don't mind. Can you jump a car with a motorcycle, though?"

"I don't know. I've never tried. I was talking about my truck."

He had an old blue pickup truck, she knew. He drove that on the frequent days of rain along the Oregon Coast.

"Right."

"Let's take a look first under the hood. Can you pop it for me?"

She fumbled beneath the steering wheel to find the right lever that would release the hood, then climbed out just as Wes was taking off his leather jacket and setting it on the seat of his motorcycle.

The plain black T-shirt he wore underneath showed off muscular biceps and the tattoos that adorned them.

As he bent over the engine, worn jeans hugging his behind, his T-shirt rode up slightly, revealing a few inches of his muscular back. Her stomach tingled and Jenna swallowed and looked away, appalled at herself for having an instinctive reaction to a man who left her so jumpy.

"Yep. Looks like you need a new battery. I'll give you a quick jump so you can make it to work. If you want, I can pick up another battery and put it in for you this evening."

Jenna tried not to gape at him. Why was he being so nice to her, when she hadn't exactly thrown out the welcome mat for him?

"I… That would be very kind. Thank you."

"Give me a second to pull my truck around."

"What's wrong with the car? Is it broken?" Addie asked from the back seat after Wes moved to his pickup truck and climbed inside, then started doing multiple-point turns to put it in position for jumper cables to reach her battery from his.

"The battery is dead. Our nice neighbor Mr. Calhoun is going to try to help us get it started."

"I can't be late today. I have to give my book report first thing."

"Hopefully we can still make it in time," she answered, as Wes turned off his truck and released the hood latch, then climbed out, rummaged behind the seats for some jumper cables and started hooking things up.

"What do I need to do?" she asked, feeling awkward and clueless. She had needed to have a vehicle jumped a few times before, early in her marriage, but Ryan had always taken care of those kind of things for her. She should have paid more attention to the process.

"Nothing yet. I'll tell you when to try starting it again."

He hooked up the cables, then fired up his truck before coming back to her car. "Okay. Let's give it a go and see what happens."

Mentally crossing her fingers, she pushed the ignition button. To her vast relief, the engine turned for a second or two, then burst into life.

"Yay!" Addie exclaimed. "Does that mean we don't have to walk to school?"

"We would have found a ride somehow," Jenna assured her. "But it looks like we've been rescued, thanks to Mr. Calhoun."

"Thanks, Mr. Calhoun. I have to give a report this morning on a book about bees and didn't want to be late."

"You're very welcome. You can call me Wes, by the way. You don't have to call me Mr. Calhoun."

Her daughter beamed at him, unfazed by that hard, unsmiling face. "Thanks, Wes."

"You can as well," he said to Jenna. Their gazes met and she couldn't help noticing how long his dark eyelashes were, an odd contrast to the hard planes of his features.

"Thank you, Wes," she forced herself to say. "I really appreciate the help."

"It was no problem. I'll grab a battery for you today. Do you have jumper cables, in case your car doesn't start after you're done at school today?"

She was relieved she could answer in the affirmative. "Yes. I have an emergency kit in back with flares, a flashlight and a blanket, along with a few tools and jumper cables."

"Good. With any luck, you might not need them."

"Thanks again for all your help."

He shrugged. "It's the kind of thing neighbors do for each other, right?"

His words filled her with guilt. She hadn't been very neighborly in the two weeks since he had moved in. She hadn't taken any goodies over to welcome him and did little more than nod politely in passing.

Was he being ironic? Had he noticed how she went out of her way to avoid him whenever possible?

She hoped he didn't notice how her face flushed with heat as she mustered a smile that faded quickly as she backed out of the driveway and turned in the direction of school.

Wes watched his pretty neighbor maneuver her little blue SUV onto the road toward the elementary school.

When he was certain her vehicle wasn't going to conk out on the road, he returned his pickup to its customary spot and climbed back onto his Harley.

It might be easier to take the truck today but he was in the mood for a bike ride, which was just about the only thing that could do anything at all to calm his restlessness.

That was an odd turn for his morning to take, but he was happy to help out, even if Jenna Haynes looked at him out of those big blue eyes like she was afraid he was about to drag her by her hair up the stairs to his apartment and lock her in his sex dungeon.

He might have found her skittishness a little amusing if he hadn't spent the past three years in company with people capable of that and so much worse.

It still burned under his skin how she and others considered him. An ex-con. Not an innocent man wrongfully convicted because of a betrayal that still burned but someone who had probably been exactly where he belonged. Even if he hadn't done the particular crime that had put him behind bars, he was no doubt guilty of *something*, right?

He hated it, that pearl-clutching, self-righteous, condemnatory attitude he had encountered since his release. After two months on the outside, he was still trying to adjust to the knowledge that his slate would never be wiped completely clean, no matter how many neighborly things he did.

He couldn't be bothered by what Jenna Haynes thought of him. What anybody thought of him. He had clung to sanity in prison by remembering that he was not the man others saw when they looked at him.

He lifted his face to the sun for just a moment before shoving on his helmet. He couldn't get enough of feeling the warmth of it on his face or smelling air scented with spring and the sea.

Clutch your pearls all you want, Ms. Haynes, he thought. *I'm alive and free. That's enough for today.*

He drove his bike through light traffic to Cannon Beach Car and Bike Repair, the garage where he had been lucky to find a job after showing up in town with mainly his bike, his truck and the small settlement he had received from the state of Illinois.

He had just parked the bike and was taking off his helmet when a tall, dark-haired and very pregnant woman climbed out of a silver sedan and hurried over to him.

Wes sighed and braced himself, not at all in the mood to have a confrontation with his ex-wife that morning. Though they had a generally friendly relationship, he couldn't imagine why she would show up unless she was mad about something. Not when she could have called or texted for anything benign.

"There you are," Lacey exclaimed. "I thought you started work at eight."

He looked at his watch that read eight oh five. "I had a neighbor with a dead battery. It took me a minute to get the car started. What's up? Have you been waiting for me? You could have called."

"I know. But I had to run next door anyway to pick up something at the hardware store after I dropped off Brielle at school, so I figured I would stop here first to talk to you while I was out."

He really hoped she wasn't about to tell him her husband had been transferred again, after only being moved here a year ago to become manager of a chain department store in a nearby town.

Wes liked it here in Cannon Beach. He liked running on the beach in the mornings and sitting in the gardens of Brambleberry House in the evenings to watch the sun slide into the water.

He liked his job, too. He had worked in a neighborhood auto mechanic shop all through high school and summers during college and definitely knew his way around an engine, motorcycle or car.

Did he want to do it forever? No. As much as he had admired and respected the neighbor who had employed him—and all those who worked with their hands—Wes didn't think working as a mechanic was his destiny. He still didn't know what he wanted to do as he worked toward rebuilding the life that had been taken from him. But for now he had found a good place, working with honest, hardworking people who cared about treating their customers right.

It paid the bills and was challenging enough not to bore him, but not overwhelming as he tried to ease back into outside life.

"What's going on?"

He could see his boss, Carlos Gutierrez, and his brother Paco watching them through the small front window of the shop.

"You know you don't always have to cut to the chase, right?" Lacey looked exasperated. "We're not having a quick conversation between prison bars anymore. A little small talk would be fine. You could say *hi, Lacey. How are you? How's the house? How's the baby?*"

Wes worked to keep his expression neutral. He

might have agreed with her, except their marriage hadn't exactly been filled with small talk, even before his arrest.

"How are you feeling?" he asked. He had learned a long time ago it was best to try humoring her whenever possible.

Lacey was a devoted, loving mother to their daughter and he still considered her a dear friend. If circumstances had been different, he would have tried like hell to keep their marriage together.

Still, he couldn't help being more than a little grateful her sometimes volatile moods were another man's problems these days.

"I'm good. Huge. I can't believe I still have ten weeks to go before the baby comes."

They had been divorced for two and a half years. She had remarried her childhood sweetheart a year almost to the day their divorce had been finalized and was now expecting a son with Ron Summers.

Wes was happy for her. When he had little to do but think about his life, it hadn't taken long for Wes to recognize that his marriage to Lacey had been a mistake from start to finish. He had been twenty-one, about to head off overseas with the army, and she had been eighteen and desperate to escape an unhappy home life, with an abusive father and neglectful mother.

They hadn't been a good fit for each other. He could

see that now, though both of them had spent years trying to deny the inevitable.

One good thing had come out of it. One amazing thing, actually. His nine-year-old daughter, Brielle. She was his heart, his purpose, his everything.

"That's actually why I'm here. Ron has the chance to take a last-minute trip to Costa Rica for work. He'll be gone ten days and he wants me to go with him, if I can swing it. This is my last chance to travel for a while, at least until the baby is older."

"Sounds like fun," he said, trying to figure out where he came in and why she had accosted him at his workplace to deliver the news.

"The problem is that I can't take Brie. She doesn't have a passport and there's no way to get one for her in time."

Ah. Now things were beginning to make sense.

"Is there any chance she could come stay with you while we're gone?"

A host of complications ran through his head, starting with the building just beyond her. The Gutierrez brothers had been good to him. He couldn't just leave them in the lurch to facilitate his ex-wife's travel plans.

He worked full-time and would have to arrange childcare. Brielle was nine going on eighteen and likely thought she was fully capable of being on her own while he worked all day. Wes definitely didn't agree.

But he couldn't bring her down here to the garage with him all day, either.

He would figure that part out later. How could he turn down the chance to spend as much time as possible with his daughter, considering all the years he had missed?

"Sure. Of course. I would love to have her."

Lacey's face lit up with happiness, reminding him with painful clarity that it had been a long time since they had been able to make each other happy.

"Oh, that's amazing. Thank you! Brie will be so excited when I tell her. The alternative was staying with my friend Shandy and she has that five-year-old who can be a real pistol. Brielle will much prefer staying with her dad."

He could only hope he was up to the task. "When do you leave?" Wes asked.

"Next Friday. The last day of school."

It would have been easier if she were leaving during the school year, when he would only need to arrange after-school care until his shift was over, but he would figure things out.

He couldn't say no. He had moved to Cannon Beach, following Lacey and her new family in order to nurture his relationship with Brielle. He couldn't miss what seemed to be a glorious opportunity to be with her.

"No problem. We'll have a great time."

"You're the best. Seriously. Thanks, Wes."

She stood on tiptoe and kissed his cheek, and as her mouth brushed his cheek, Wes couldn't help wishing that things could have worked out differently between them.

He couldn't honestly say he regretted the end of a marriage that had been troubled from the beginning. He did regret that the decisions made by the adults in Brielle's life complicated things for her, forcing her to now split her time between them.

"You do remember that today is Guest Lunch at the school, right? Brie said you were planning to go. If you're not, I'm sure Ron could swing by on his lunch break."

He really tried not to feel competitive with his daughter's stepfather, who seemed overall like a good guy, if a little on the superficial side.

"I'll be there," he answered, hoping the day wouldn't be inordinately busy at the shop.

The Gutierrez brothers were great to work with, but an employer could only be so understanding.

As he watched his ex-wife drive away, the second time he had been caught in the wake of a woman's taillights that morning, he was reminded of Jenna Haynes and her car trouble.

If he were swinging by the school anyway for lunch, he might as well take a car battery with him and fix Jenna Haynes's car. It was an easy ten-minute job, and that way she wouldn't have to worry about the possibility of it not starting after school.

He told himself the little burst of excitement was only the anticipation of doing a nice, neighborly deed. It had nothing to do with the knowledge that he would inevitably see Jenna again.

Chapter Two

"Stay in line, class. Remember, hands to yourself."

Jenna did her best to steer her class of twenty-three third-grade students—including three with special learning needs and Individualized Education Programs—into the lunchroom with a minimum of distractions.

The day that had started out with such stunning news from Angela had quickly spiraled. Her dead battery had only been the beginning.

As soon as she reached the school, she discovered both of her paraprofessionals, who helped with reading and math, as well as giving extra attention to those who struggled most, had called in for personal leave. One was pregnant and had bad morning sickness and the other one had to travel out of town at the last minute to be with a dying relative.

Jenna completely understood they both had excellent reasons to be gone. Unfortunately, that left her to handle the entire class by herself, and her third-grade students were so jacked up over the approaching summer vacation—or maybe the sugar in her cupcakes—that none of them seemed able to focus.

One more week, she told herself. One more week and then she would have the entire summer to herself.

The previous summer, she had taken classes all summer to finish her master's degree, as well as working nearly full-time at Rosa's gift shop, By-the-Wind.

She didn't feel as if she had enjoyed any summer vacation at all.

She wasn't going to make that mistake again this year. Though she still had two more classes to go before earning her master's degree, she had decided to hold off until after the summer and she had told Rosa she couldn't work as many hours at the gift shop.

Addie was growing up and Jenna wanted to spend as much time as possible with her daughter while Addie still seemed to like being with her.

"Don't want spaghetti." The sudden strident shout from one of her students, Cody Andrews, drew looks from several students in the cafeteria. Some of the adult guests having lunch with their students also gave the boy the side-eye.

Jenna felt immediately on the defensive. Cody, who had been diagnosed with autism, was an eager, funny, bright student, but sometimes crowds could set him off and trigger negative behaviors.

He had seemed to have a particularly difficult morning, maybe because Monica, the aide he loved dearly, wasn't there.

"Do you want to get pizza from the à la carte line?" she asked him, her voice low and calming.

"No. I don't like pizza." That was news to her, since his favorite food was usually pizza and he could eat it five days a week without a fuss.

"What about chicken tenders?"

He appeared to consider that for a long moment, his blond head tilted and his brow furrowed. Finally he nodded. "Okay. I like tenders."

The lunchroom was crowded with parents and friends of the students who had come for their monthly Lunch with a Guest activity.

She strongly suspected another of the reasons for Cody's outburst might have something to do with that. His parents were recently divorced, and his father, who used to come have lunch with him every month, had moved two towns over.

Normally she didn't eat with the students, preferring to grab a quick bite at her desk while they were out at recess, unless she was on playground duty. But because Cody was being so clingy, she had decided to bring her sack lunch to the table. Now he slid in next to her with his tray of nuggets.

She waved to a few of the parents, then pulled out her sandwich just as she felt the presence of someone behind her.

She turned and was astonished to discover her upstairs neighbor standing beside his daughter, Brielle. He was holding a tray that carried both their lunches.

"Hello."

In boots, jeans and the same black T-shirt he had been wearing earlier in the day, he looked big and tough and intimidating. Completely out of place in an elementary school lunchroom.

He should moonlight as a bouncer at a biker bar, since nobody would dare mess with him.

"Hi, Mrs. Haynes. This is my dad." Brielle, his daughter, beamed with pride.

"I know. I've met him. We're neighbors."

"This is his very first time coming to one of the Lunch with a Guest days."

She forced a smile. "Welcome. I hope you enjoy yourself."

"So far, so good. It's pizza. What could go wrong with pizza?"

He obviously had not tried the school pizza yet, which could double as a paperweight in a pinch.

Jenna was disconcerted when Wes pointed to an empty spot down the row from her. "Is it all right if we sit here? There doesn't seem to be room with Brielle's class."

It was always a tight squeeze in the small lunchroom when each student brought a guest. Parents ended up finding spots wherever they could. She gestured to the empty spot. "Go ahead."

She was fiercely aware of him as she finished her sandwich.

"I have a dog," Cody suddenly announced. "Her

name is Jojo, and she's white and brown with ears and a brown tail. Do you want to see?"

Jenna realized with some alarm that the boy was talking to Wes in particular, unfazed by his intimidating appearance.

"Um. Sure."

Cody pulled out the small four-by-six photo album he carried with him all the time in the front pocket of his hoodie, a sort of talisman. He opened it and thrust it into Wes's face, far too close for comfort.

"Wow. She's very pretty," Wes answered.

"Does she do any tricks?" Brielle asked, genuine curiosity in her voice as she peered around her father's muscular arm to see the photograph.

"She comes when I call her and she sits and she can roll over."

"I wish we had a dog," Brielle said, a hint of sadness in her voice. "We have a cat, though, and it's the best cat in the whole world."

Jenna thought the interaction would end there, as Cody could be quiet and withdrawn with strangers. She was surprised when the boy turned the page of his well-worn photo album to show other things that were important to him in his life. His bedroom. His bicycle. His father, who had walked out the previous year.

She might have expected Wes to turn his attention back to his daughter. That was the reason he had come to lunch, after all, to spend time with Brielle. Instead, he seemed to go out of his way to include the boy in their conversation.

She couldn't help being touched and grateful for his efforts, especially because it allowed her a chance to interact with some of the other students who did not have a guest with them for various reasons.

As soon as the children finished lunch, they were each quick to return their trays to the cafeteria and rush outside for recess.

Brielle seemed to take her time over the meal, probably to spend more time with her father. Cody was the last to linger at the table, apparently enjoying his new friends too much to leave.

When he left to go out to recess, watched over by the playground aides, Jenna rose as well.

"I brought over a battery for your car," Wes said abruptly. "I can switch it out for you before I head back to the garage. I thought that might be better so you don't have to worry about needing a jump again after school is out."

This man was full of surprises. "Really? You would do that on your lunch hour?"

He shrugged. "It's no trouble. Will take me less than ten minutes. Brie can help me. She loves to work on cars, don't you?"

His daughter beamed. "Yep."

"I will need your car keys, though."

"They're in my classroom. I'm about to head back there, if you don't mind following me."

"Not a problem."

He and his daughter walked with her, Brielle chattering happily with her father. She didn't seem to mind his monosyllabic responses.

As they made their way through the halls, Jenna couldn't help but be aware of Wes. She was a little surprised to realize she had lost some of her nervousness around him. It was very difficult to remain afraid of a man who could show such kindness to a young boy who could sometimes struggle in social situations.

"Thank you for helping with Cody. He's having a pretty tough time right now. Guest days are sometimes hard on him. You helped distract him."

"I didn't do much. We just talked about his dog."

She wanted to tell him the conversation obviously meant much more to the boy, who was deeply missing his father, but she didn't want to get into Cody's personal problems with him, especially not with Brielle there.

"The distraction was exactly what he needed. Thank you."

Wes didn't quite smile, but she thought his usual stern expression seemed to soften a little. "Glad I could help. About those keys..."

"Yes. I'll get them."

She opened her classroom and headed for the closet where she kept her personal effects. After digging through her purse, she pulled out her key chain with her car fob.

"Here you go," she said.

He held his hand out and she dropped the keys into it, grateful she didn't have to touch him for the handover.

"Thanks. I'll bring them back when I'm done."

"Do you need my help out there?"

"No. We got it."

"Thank you."

The words seemed inadequate but she did not know what else to say. As soon as Wes and Brielle walked out the side door closest to the faculty parking lot, her friend Kim Baker rushed out of her classroom across the hall, where she taught fifth grade.

"Who is that?" Kim asked, eyes wide. "I must know immediately."

"My neighbor."

"*That's* the serial killer?"

Jenna winced, feeling guilty that she had confided in her dear friend after she found out Wes had recently been released from prison.

"He's not a serial killer. I never said he was. He was in prison for property crimes. Fraud, extortion, theft. But Anna and Rosa assure me he was exonerated."

"There you go, then. You should be fine."

"Especially since I have nothing to steal."

"You and me both, honey. We're teachers." Kim looked in the direction Wes had gone. "I have to say, I wouldn't mind having that man on top of me."

"Kim!" she exclaimed.

"Living upstairs," her friend said with a wink. "What did you think I meant?"

She rolled her eyes. "You're a happily married woman. Not to mention soon to be a grandmother."

Kim was only in her midforties but had married and started a family young. Her daughter was following in her footsteps, married and pregnant by twenty-two.

"I am all those things, but I'm not dead. And he is way hotter than you let on, you sly thing."

Jenna could feel her face flush. She hadn't told Kim much about Wes.

"I am curious about why your sexy new neighbor is stopping by in the middle of the day to talk to you. Is there something you're not telling me?"

"No!" she exclaimed quickly. "Nothing like what you're thinking. He jumped me this morning."

"Go on," Kim said, eyes wide with exaggerated lasciviousness.

Jenna let out an exasperated laugh. "My car died, I mean. He jumped my battery. He offered to fix it tonight, but since he was coming by the school today to see his daughter for lunch, he offered to fix it now."

To her vast relief, this information was enough for Kim to drop the double entendres. "That is really nice of him."

"Yes. It is."

"And you're sure that's all?"

"Yes," she said, more forcefully this time. "He's been very kind. That's all."

Kim made a face and reached for Jenna's hand, her features suddenly serious.

"I'm only saying this as your friend, but I can't think of anyone else who deserves to have their battery jumped by a sexy guy. And if he's kind and thoughtful, all the better."

The genuine concern in her voice touched Jenna, even if she didn't agree with the sentiment. She was deeply grateful for the many friendships she had made since coming to Cannon Beach. The people of this community had truly embraced her and welcomed her and Addison into their midst.

She still could not quite believe she was now free to stay here as long as she wanted.

"I appreciate the sweet sentiment, Kim, but I'm fine. Completely fine. I have everything I need. A great apartment, a job I love, Addie. It's more than enough. I don't need a man in my life."

And especially one who intimidated her as much as Wes Calhoun.

Kim did not look convinced, but before her friend could argue, Wes returned to Jenna's classroom, on his own this time instead of with his daughter.

He set Jenna's keys on the edge of her desk. "Here you go. She's running great now. Started right up. Looks like you're due for an oil change, though. You're going to want to get on that."

"I will. Thanks. What do I owe you for the battery?"

He looked reluctant to give a number but finally

did, something that seemed far less than she was expecting.

"What about labor?"

"Nothing. There was really no labor involved."

She wanted to argue but couldn't figure out how in a gracious way. "Thank you, then," she finally said. "I'm very grateful."

She would have said more, but the bell rang in that moment and children began to swarm back into the classroom from the playground.

"Glad I could help," he answered. "I'll let you get back to your students."

"I'll settle up with you this evening, if that's okay."

Again she had the impression he wanted to tell her not to worry about it, but he finally nodded. "Sounds good. See you later."

Two students approached her desk to ask a question about the field trip they were taking on Monday to the aquarium in Lincoln City. By the time she answered them, Wes had slipped away.

Don't miss
A Beach House Beginning
by RaeAnne Thayne,
available August 2024 wherever
Harlequin Special Edition books
and ebooks are sold.
www.Harlequin.com